# TARGET PRACTICE

Fargo hit the floor. Bullets flew over his head. His first shot, from underneath, tore at the nearest man's belly. The second caught the other man in the chest. He flew backward as though kicked by a mule.

Fargo vaulted through the open window. The third man was draping Isabella over the saddle of a horse. "Don't move!" Fargo shouted. As he expected, the man did the opposite. He whirled and drew his gun. As he did so, he moved a few inches away from the girl. . . .

Fargo took the chance. One way or another, Isabella would be set free. His Colt roared. . . .

# THE TRAILSMAN

106

# SIERRA SHOOTOUT

by

## Jon Sharpe

A SIGNET BOOK

SIGNET
Published by the Penguin Group
Penguin Books USA Inc., 375 Hudson Street,
New York, New York 10014, U.S.A.
Penguin Books Ltd, 27 Wrights Lane,
London W8 5TZ, England
Penguin Books Australia Ltd, Ringwood,
Victoria, Australia
Penguin Books Canada Ltd, 2801 John Street,
Markham, Ontario, Canada L3R 1B4
Penguin Books (N.Z.) Ltd, 182-190 Wairau Road,
Auckland 10, New Zealand

Penguin Books Ltd, Registered Offices:
Harmondsworth, Middlesex, England

First published by Signet, an imprint of New American Library, a division
of Penguin Books USA Inc.

First Printing, October, 1990
10  9  8  7  6  5  4  3  2  1

The first chapter of this book previously appeared in *Black Hills Blood*,
the one hundred and fifth volume in this series.

 REGISTERED TRADEMARK—MARCA REGISTRADA

Printed in the United States of American

PUBLISHER'S NOTE
This is a work of fiction. Names, characters, places, and incidents either
are the product of the author's imagination or are used fictitiously, and any
resemblance to actual persons, living or dead, events, or locales is entirely
coincidental.

# The Trailsman

Beginnings . . . they bend the tree and they mark the man. Skye Fargo was born when he was eighteen. Terror was his midwife, vengeance his first cry. Killing spawned Skye Fargo, ruthless, cold-blooded murder. Out of the acrid smoke of gunpowder still hanging in the air, he rose, cried out a promise never forgotten.

The Trailsman they began to call him all across the West: searcher, scout, hunter, the man who could see where others only looked, his skills for hire but not his soul, the man who lived each day to the fullest, yet trailed each tomorrow. Skye Fargo, the Trailsman, the seeker who could take the wildness of a land and the wanting of a woman and make them his own.

*1861, the great Sierra Nevada Range in California, a land where murderers and missionaries, soldiers and seekers, have crossed paths since the sixteenth century . . .*

# 1

The big man sat very straight astride the magnificent black-and-white Ovaro as he stared down at the raging river below. His lake-blue eyes narrowed on the two figures at the edge of the river beside a small, short rowboat. "Goddamn, they're going to try to cross," he muttered aloud, awe in his voice.

His eyes flicked back to the river and saw the raging torrent of brownish water that raced at breakneck speed. The sun was bright and hot now, but the river was swollen by the torrential rains that had left him holed up in a cave for two days.

The big man's chiseled jaw was a hard line as he leaned forward in the saddle to peer at the two figures again, one a gray-haired man in a loose-fitting peasant shirt, the other a young woman with thick black hair and a white blouse.

She was plainly trying to keep the older man from climbing into the rowboat. That showed she had sense. The clumsy rowboat would never survive the raging waters. But even as the thought tumbled through his mind, he saw the man shake the girl off and step into the rowboat. He picked up one of the oars and began to push the boat into the water. The young woman followed him into the boat and took up the other oar.

"Damn fools," Sky Fargo hissed as he sent the Ovaro down the hillside. But as he reached the shoreline, the boat was already in the water and was instantly swept downriver. He saw the young woman pulling hard on her oar as the short rowboat was sent spinning, carried along on the top of the churning water. Both the man and the girl pulled frantically to control the boat, but it was so much wasted effort as the rushing river turned the craft one way and then the other, lifted it half out of the water, and sent it crashing down again.

Fargo sent the Ovaro along the shoreline, paralleling the boat as it spun wildly out of control. It was not a question of whether or not they'd survive, but only of how long before they were killed. The answer took less than a minute as Fargo saw the boat caught between two rushing, bubbling torrents of water, lifted and upended as if by a giant, invisible hand. Both the girl and the man were blurred, dark objects as they arched through the air and disappeared into the river.

Fargo drew his lariat from the fork swell of his saddle as he came abreast of the overturned rowboat. He glimpsed the young woman surface; she managed to get one hand on the boat only to slide off instantly, disappear, and surface again. Her arms flailed against the swirling water as she fought desperately to stay afloat, and once again she managed to bring one hand alongside the boat.

Fargo raised the lariat, shouted, and saw her head turn as he sent the rope whirling through the air. The loop came down along the overturned bottom of the boat and skittered alongside the girl. He saw her close both hands on it just as she lost her hold on the boat.

"Get it around one shoulder," he shouted, aware

**10**

that she'd never be able to slip the loop over her head and shoulders in the tossing turbulence. He saw her pull the loop over one shoulder and he pulled it tight at once. She curled both hands around the rope. He moved the Ovaro backward up the shoreline and watched the girl's body buffeted by the raging water, twisted back and forth as he pulled her along the surface of the river. She clung to the lariat with dogged desperation, the rope truly a lifeline. Finally he pulled her onto the shore and leapt from the saddle as she raised herself on one elbow and spit out mouthfuls of the river.

Her black hair lay plastered tight against her head, but even the river hadn't taken the dense curls out of it. He saw a round face, attractive enough, a wide mouth and slightly broad nose, a face that youth prevented from being coarse. A soaked white blouse lay hard against deep, heavy breasts, which heaved as she gasped for air. "That was one damn fool thing to do," Fargo rasped.

"Pedro . . . my uncle, try to find him," she said. "Please. Maybe he is still swimming."

"You stay here," Fargo said. He wheeled the Ovaro and sent the horse racing downriver, the act more a gesture than a hope. He came in sight of the rowboat, still wildly spinning, some fifty yards on. He'd ridden another fifty when a shout of surprise welled up from his throat. The man's body lay wedged into the tangled branches of a partly submerged, dead tree along the opposite bank. The racing waters pulled on the man, dragging his legs out at an angle that made it certain he'd be dislodged in minutes.

Fargo reined to a halt and dropped to the ground, the lariat in his hands again. The river had narrowed, not much yet enough to give him a chance at reaching the opposite shore. He wasn't even certain the figure still breathed, but using all the power of his back and shoulder muscles, he sent the lariat sailing across the top of the churning river. He grunted in satisfaction as the rope landed on the branches and half across the figure.

The man's head lifted as the rope struck him across the back. "Under your arms," Fargo shouted. "Put it under your arms." He watched as, with agonizing slowness, the man managed to secure the rope around himself. Fargo pulled, gently at first, then harder as the rope tightened and the man slid from the tangled branches and back into the river. The Trailsman felt the impact on his arms and shoulders as the rushing water frantically grasped and tugged, the river unwilling to give up a victim.

Fargo, heels dug hard into the soft earth of the bank, pulled the man toward him and had his prize almost at midriver when three horsemen suddenly appeared along the oposite bank. They came to a halt and Fargo frowned as he saw rifles suddenly appear in the hands of the three riders.

His jaw dropped open as he saw them raise their rifles and fire. Three bullets thudded into the man in the water and Fargo felt the lariat grow limp. He realized he was still staring in disbelief, feeling as though he'd been suddenly plunged into a wild and unreal dream. But the three horsemen were very real as they started to race away.

"Goddamn," Fargo bit out. He held on to the lariat with his left hand as he drew his own big Colt .44. He fired across the river, shots flung off in a half-vacuum of shock and disbelief that missed as the three horsemen raced out of sight. He holstered his gun and returned to pulling on the lariat until he brought the now-lifeless form ashore. He stared down at the short gray-haired man while a mixture of feeling helpless and cheated quivered inside him.

But it was plain now why the man had elected to risk the churning waters of the rain-swollen river. He was fleeing for his life. Fargo frowned as the young woman came into his thoughts. Had she, too, been running for her life?

He gathered up his lariat, swung onto the pinto, and rode back along the shore. The young woman rose to her feet as she saw him. He dismounted as he halted in front of her. The wet blouse still clung, he saw, outlining a large, dark circle at the tip of each deep breast.

Her black-brown eyes peered at him with concern. "I heard shots," she said.

"You did," Fargo said grimly, and told her what had happened.

She sank to her knees in the soft sand of the riverbank to sway back and forth in a rocking motion, both arms crossed over her breasts, and tiny moaning sounds came from her full lips. "My God, oh, my God . . . *Dios mío*," she said.

"Suppose you tell me what this is all about?" Fargo said. "You said he was your uncle."

"Yes, Pedro Santas. I am Magdalena Santas," the young woman said as she pushed to her feet.

"Why were you running?" Fargo questioned.

"He was. I wanted to stop him. But he wouldn't listen," Magdalena Santas said, and Fargo remembered how she'd plainly been arguing with her uncle beside the boat. "When he got into the boat, I had to go with him. I had to try to help him go downriver and get away."

"Who were those three men?" Fargo questioned.

"I don't know."

"Your uncle didn't tell you why he was running?"

13

"Only that he saw something," Magdalena said. "He saw something and he had to run."

"That's all?"

The girl nodded. "He came rushing home, his face white as a sun-bleached bone. I asked him what he had seen, but he wouldn't tell me. He was almost in shock. He kept saying it was *malo, muy malo . . .* very bad," she said. "I asked him to tell me what it was he'd seen, but he told me it was best I didn't know. He said that if I knew, I'd be in danger. That's all he said as he tried to pack some clothes in a sack. He gave up and just ran."

"And you followed," Fargo put in.

"Yes, naturally. Tío Pedro raised me from a little girl. We shared our home. He was like a father to me," Magdalena said, her voice breaking.

Fargo reached out, closed a hand over her shoulder, wet and soft under the blouse. "I'm sorry," he said. "Whatever it was, somebody knew he'd seen it."

She nodded, her eyes closed. "They probably went to the house first," she said.

"And realized he'd run. They found a way to cross the river, probably upland, and rode down looking for him. Another minute and I'd have had him ashore alive," Fargo said, bitterness in his voice.

Magdalena Santas opened her eyes and turned to him. He saw the stolid resignation in her face. "A minute spells a lifetime," she said. "Bring him to me, please. There is a cemetery behind the village. It is the place for him to be."

Fargo nodded, his lips a grim line as he climbed onto the horse and retraced his steps down the shoreline. When he returned, he was on foot, the body of Pedro Santas draped across the pinto's saddle.

Magdalena fell in step beside him and led the way through low hills and rolling land with thick stands of

*14*

hawthorn and white alder. "I do not know your name, big man," she said as she walked beside him.

"Fargo . . . Skye Fargo," the Trailsman answered.

"You are not from here," Magdalena said.

"That's right." Fargo smiled. "How did you know?"

"You have a different way to you," she said. "And that *caballo magnífico* of yours, I have never seen such a horse around here. Our horses are very fine, but they are mostly out of Arab and Morgan stock."

"Your uncle raised horses?"

"No, no, but you cannot live in the Sierras without learning something about horses," Magdalena said.

"How far to the village?"

"Soon," she said.

He cast a glance at the sky where the afternoon sun had begun to slide toward the horizon. He brought his eyes back to Magdalena Santas. She walked with a firm step, deep breasts swaying, youth giving a firm vigor to her full figure. Only her face showed the quiet pain inside her.

They turned a curve and he saw the low hill with the small stone houses, not so much a village as a collection of dwellings shouldering one another. Men and women came from the houses, and Magdalena spoke to them in a mixture of Spanish and English. Three men stepped forward and took the body from the Ovaro.

Fargo noticed the row of crosses at the top of the hill.

Magdalena turned to him as a small procession formed and began to move up the hill. "Will you wait?" she asked.

"Yes. There are things to say," Fargo answered.

"For me, also," Magdalena said, and hurried after the others.

Fargo turned away, lowered himself onto a flat

**15**

rock, and let his gaze move out across the vast land. The massive mountains of the Sierra Nevada rose up in the north, rolling hills and high plateaus stretched to the west. Far to the south, the land became vast, arid deserts. It was a land of contrasts, this California, rugged beauty in all its varied faces, a state with proper borders that butted against the vast and sprawling Oregon Territory.

The Spaniards had come first, conquerors and explorers, and claimed the land for the Spanish kings. The great trek of missionaries had followed, the Franciscans, Jesuits, Dominicans, Benedictines, and still more, conquerors and explorers in their own way. It began in the sixteenth century, the new land established by the Spaniards, and stayed that way until 1822, when California changed its allegiance to Mexico. Then a group of settlers revolted and claimed an independent republic. Soon after, the Mexican-American War broke out and California was ceded to America. But before it became a state, the first real American influence came to the land when gold was discovered and thousands rushed from every state and territory to become gold rich overnight. Only a few succeeded, Fargo recalled with a wry snort, and many died before even reaching their goal.

But despite the gold rush and the wild and disparate horde it brought, the Mexican and Spanish heritage stayed deep in the land and its people. He was a stranger here. The land was new to him, but new lands and new trails were the way of a trailsman, a way that was as much from within as without. Knowledge and skill were things learned. Sensitivity and insight were things given. Together, they let him see where other men only looked, listen when others could only hear, and know when other men wondered. It was the reputation of his skills that had brought the letter to him at the Bundy ranch, where he had broken trail for a special herd all the way from Oklahoma to Utah. The letter had asked him to come without commitment, contained directions and the kind of travel money a man would be a fool to turn down. So he had come to the Far West land they called California, curiosity more than anything else his silent saddle companion.

He let idle thoughts trail away and rose to his feet as he saw the small procession start down the hillside.

Magdalena came to him, her blouse almost dried out now, to rest against her with more propriety. "Come home with me. We can talk there. My house is on the other side of the hill," she said.

He nodded and pulled her onto the Ovaro with him; she rode in silence as he enjoyed the well-fleshed warmth of her against him in the saddle. She guided him to a small stone house, alone on the back of the hillside. Mexican in style, it looked much the same as the others he had seen. She slid from the saddle and her heavy breasts bounced as she touched the ground.

"I'll put my horse around the back," Fargo said, and she waited while he rode to the rear of the house. Under an overhang, he found a small brown mare and a two-wheeled, wooden road cart, a heavier, less graceful version of the light eastern model. He put the Ovaro under the overhang, and when he walked back to the front of the house, Magdalena was waiting in the open doorway. He followed her into a fair-sized living room with stone walls and braided mats on the floor, a worn settee and a stuffed chair. The house was clean and neat, and he spied a kitchen and two other rooms in the rear.

Magdalena turned a lamp on as dusk began to settle over the hillside. "I offer you this house to stay the night or as long as you wish. It is so little for what you did for me and tried to do for Pedro."

"I was figuring to spend the night," Fargo said, and smiled at the mixture of surprise and uncertainty that came into the young woman's black-brown eyes. "The men who shot your uncle don't know what he might have told you," he said, and watched relief and gratefulness wipe away the surprise.

"They might come back for me?"

"There's a chance," he said, and her hand reached out and closed around his arm.

"Thank you for thinking of that. You are a special man, Skye Fargo."

"It's called experience," he said, smiling.

"It's called being wonderful," she said, and pulled him down on the worn settee with her. "Who are you, Fargo? What brings you to California?"

"Some call me the Trailsman," he answered. "A man out here sent for me. I'd guess he wants what I do best." He paused, let himself take in the firm, youthful attractiveness of Magdalena Santas, the earth part of her. Her peasant roots gave her an open, guileless honesty that was part of her direct, dark eyes. "Did you help your uncle work the land here?" he asked.

Her smile was lovely even when tinged with wistfulness, as it was now. "No, Uncle Pedro was a builder, something like what you call a stonemason. He built many of the houses you saw on the hill. For many years, when I was a little girl, he worked for the friars at the Mission of Santa Angelica. He built much of the mission, along with the brothers, of course," she said.

"So what does Magdalena Santas do in this wild land?"

"I work as a housemaid for one of the wealthy ranchers in the valley, Philip Rogers," she said, and Fargo's brows lifted.

"Philip Rogers is the man that sent for me," he told her.

Anticipation rushed into her surprised expression. "This *is* something! Quite a coincidence," Magdalena said. "Then maybe you will be staying awhile."

"Can't say," Fargo told her. "Tell me more about Philip Rogers." He leaned forward and turned out the lamp, and the room plunged into darkness. "We don't need light to talk."

"I understand," she murmured, and he let a few moments pass for his eyes to grow accustomed to the darkness. Finally Magdelena took shape again, a soft, dark outline as a sliver of moonlight threaded its way through a window to supply the faintest of light. "Philip Rogers is maybe the richest of some seven or eight ranchers who live in the valley just north of here. He breeds and sells fancy horses, pure-bred Arab stock, and sends them north as far as Cape Mendocino," she said. In the darkness, her voice seemed to take on a huskier quality. "But there has been much trouble for the last few months around here."

"What kind of trouble?"

"*Bandidos*," Magdalena said. "Very smart *bandidos*, it seems. They have been raiding the ranches and somehow disappearing after each raid. There have been killings and other terrible things."

Fargo heard the quick shudder that came into her voice. "Only the rich ranchers?" he questioned.

"There is no one else here with anything to steal," Magdalena said, a simple acceptance in her voice.

"Maybe Philip Rogers wants me to take his fancy herd to a safer place for now," Fargo said. "Guess I'll be finding out, come tomorrow. If you go to work there every day, it can't be far away."

"An hour by my roadcart, less by horseback," she

said. "You will meet the beautiful Isabel, I'm sure," she added.

"His wife?"

"His daughter."

"Isabel," Fargo repeated. "She is of Mexican blood, like yourself?"

"Hah," Magdalena snapped. "She would have your head for that. Her mother was Spanish, pure Castillian, I am told, from a royal family."

"I take it you don't like Isabel Rogers."

"Was it that plain in my voice?" Magdalena asked, alarm and apology in her tone.

"That plain." He nodded.

"Envy," Magdalena said with disarming honesty.

"Is that all?"

"No," she said, her voice growing crisp again. "An aristocrat is supposed to have good manners, even a spoiled and rich one. You do not have to look down on everyone."

"Is that what she does?"

"She has a way, an air. She is entitled to it. I am entitled not to like it," Magdalena said.

"You are," Fargo said, and suddenly his hand shot out and closed gently over Magdalena's mouth. All the while he had talked, laughed, and listened, a part of him had been elsewhere, tuned to the night sounds outside the house, a part of the wild-creature instincts he had made part of his own. He had caught the soft sound of a hoof, and now another one came to his ears. "Company," he whispered to Magdalena, his face closer to hers.

She nodded, and he withdrew his hand and felt her clasp his arm.

# 2

Fargo listened for the sound of another hoofbeat but heard none. They must have dismounted. He brought his face alongside the softness of Magdalena's cheek. "Stay on the floor. Crawl to your room, close the door, and stay there," he whispered, and she immediately began to slide along the floor. He watched her till she disappeared into the darkness of the adjoining room before he went to the window.

He crouched by the sill and peered outside. There wasn't much cover on the hillside, some scrub brush and a cluster of hawthorn three-quarters of the way up the hill. They'd have to move into the open to reach the house, and he waited, one hand on the butt of the big Colt at his side.

The moon had risen high enough to throw a pale-silver light across the hill. Suddenly he saw a figure step from the thicket of hawthorn. His eyes moved to the other side of the low thicket and saw a second figure emerge. A third one came into sight but stayed at the edge of the hawthorns as the other two moved into the open. The first two began to move toward the house, staying some dozen feet apart, one approaching the door from the right, the other from the left. The third one stayed in the thicket, Fargo noted. He wanted one alive and able to answer questions, but he knew that was little more than a slim hope. They had killed Magdalena's uncle with merciless efficiency. Their kind didn't easily surrender.

But he'd try, he vowed, and drew the big Colt as the two men neared the house. The third remained at the edge of the thicket, little more than a shadowy shape.

Fargo cursed their cunning cautiousness. The first two had almost reached the house, and the Trailsman caught the glint of moonlight on the six-guns in their hands. He moved from the window and dropped to one knee, the Colt leveled at the doorway. He'd take out the first one and then wing the second, he planned. He heard the two men reach the door and turn the knob. The door swung inward and the first figure stepped into the house.

Fargo fired, the shot not unlike a cannon's roar inside the room, and the figure flew backward through the doorway. Fargo saw the second knocked aside as he turned to flee back down the hill. Fargo stepped into the doorway, aimed low, and fired. The man sprawled forward with a curse of pain as he clutched at his leg.

A shot rang out, splintered the edge of the doorway, and Fargo dropped low. Another shot came from the hawthorns, this one slamming into the side of the house. Fargo flattened himself on the floor in the deep shadows of the doorway and saw the second man pulling himself along the ground, moving down the hillside toward the hawthorns.

"Hold it there," he shouted. "I don't want to kill you." But the man kept crawling downhill and Fargo aimed, fired from his prone position, and another shot tore into the man's leg. He heard the man's scream of pain as he stopped and clutched at his leg again.

"Jesus," the man cried out, half-turned on his side, and cursed again.

"Stay there and you stay alive," Fargo called to him, and saw the man's head lift to peer back at the house. He started to call to the man again when the two shots rang out from the hawthorns.

Fargo flattened himself only to see that the shots hadn't come his way. Instead, he saw the figure halfway down the hillside shudder, half-rise, and then fall, to lay still. "Son of a bitch," Fargo swore. He scooted back into the darkness of the house and rose to his feet. Gathering all the power in his leg muscles, he flung himself through the doorway in a headlong dive. He was rolling when he hit the ground and continued to roll until he came up against the deep shadows at the side of the house. He stayed flat, but no more shots came from the hawthorns. Instead, he heard the unmistakable sound of a man running through the thicket. Fargo rose and started to race down the hillside, his ears trained on the sounds coming from the thicket.

When the sounds abruptly stopped, the Trailsman was ready and he hit the ground in a headlong dive as two bullets swept over his head. The sounds from the thicket came again and Fargo rose, raced downhill. An oath fell from his lips as he heard the sound of hoofbeats. He reached the hawthorns and skidded to a halt as the galloping hoofbeats faded into the distance. He holstered the Colt, swore softly to himself, and began to trudge up the hillside. He paused at the first figure on the ground, quickly rifled through the man's pockets, found nothing, and sent the inert form rolling down the hill with a kick. He did the same with the other man outside the door and finally stepped into the house.

"It's over, Magdalena," he called. "Come out."

The door to the other room opened and he caught the figure that flew into his arms. She held him close, relief and thankfulness in her grip, but there was no trembling in her. "You were right. They came back," she murmured. "Thank God you were here."

"One got away," he told her.

"Will he come back again?" she asked, alarm quick to seize her voice.

"No, he's thanking his luck now," Fargo said. "I tossed the other two down the hill."

"I'll have the men from the village take them away in the morning," Magdelena said, and stepped back. "What, now?" she asked.

"I'd say it's time to get some sleep," Fargo said, and she nodded.

"Yes, I feel as if I'd been turned inside out," she said, and led him into the adjoining room, where he saw a low bed that seemed little more than a padded mattress. "It is much more comfortable than it looks," she said as she took some garments from a closet and hurried away.

She was right, Fargo noted after he'd undressed and stretched out on the bed. He was still awake when Magdalena returned, a white cotton, knee-length night-gown around her full figure. He frowned as she climbed onto the bed and curled herself against him. The surprise and rushing thoughts that caught at him were quickly dispelled as she uttered a deep sigh. "Good night, *amigo*," she said, and lay still beside him, a little-girl naturalness to her that was as disarming as it was disconcerting.

He heard her fall asleep almost instantly, and a small smile stayed on his lips as he let himself embrace sleep also.

The night passed quietly and he heard her wake with the morning. He pulled his eyes open to see her sitting up, her gaze on the smooth, muscled symmetry of his powerful body. She quickly looked away when she felt his eyes on her, and slid from the bed.

"The well is at the side of the house," she called back as she hurried away, the nightgown tight against her full rear. Fargo rose, went to the well, washed, and dressed. When he returned to the house, Magdalena was fresh and scrubbed, her black-brown eyes glistening; she wore a fresh white peasant blouse with a scoop neck that revealed the curving tops of her full breasts. "Will you ride with me to the ranch?" she asked.

"Nothing like having your own guide," Fargo said, and strode behind the house to saddle the Ovaro.

Magdalena hitched the brown mare to the road cart and he swung in beside her as she rolled downhill. She halted at the village while he waited and then moved west along a narrow road.

"Trouble, trouble everywhere, that's all there's been for the last six months," she said. "Even the good friars at the mission have been touched by it."

"The mission?" he echoed.

"*Sí*, the Mission of Santa Angelica. The friars are Franciscans and they came here in 1700. My uncle helped build the mission. I used to play there as a little girl while he worked with the friars," Magdalena explained.

"The *bandidos* have attacked the mission, too?" Fargo frowned.

"No, the friars have had their own troubles, very bad troubles. It is what I said. Trouble has been everywhere. I don't know what's happening. Even the crops are poor."

"Troubles are like bananas: they come in bunches," Fargo said. "Is the mission your place of worship?"

"Yes, and for all the poor people around here and

all those of Mexican descent. The mission has always been our church. There is always one priest with the brothers to gave the sacraments," Magdalena said, and Fargo brought the pinto closer as she turned the road cart and dipped down into a low plateau dotted with stands of Sierra juniper, white fir, and quaking aspen. A tall wrought-iron arch came into view, an entranceway marker more than a gate. An iron name-plate under the arch read:

RR—Rancho Rogers

Magdalena drove under the arch, through the wide-spread stand of fir. Fargo spotted a man under a tree some fifteen yards to the right, a rifle in his hands. Another guard appeared a few dozen yards farther, also armed with a rifle. The half-dozen buildings appeared as they emerged from the trees, and Fargo saw two more guards, these on the perimeter of a half-circle of aspen that faced the houses.

Magdalena drove to the main house, a large, impos-ing structure of redwood and stone with big, bay win-dows. Two smaller houses flanked it, then a long bunkhouse farther away and three freshly painted stables.

Three large corrals spread beyond. Fargo took in the horses running free inside each, all beautiful speci-mens, their Arabian blood instantly visible in their small, neat ears, their slightly dish faces, and the char-acteristic bulge over their foreheads the Arabs called the *jibbah*.

Magdalena steered the road cart to one side of the house and paused to turn her eyes to him. "My home is yours to use, Fargo," she said. "You can sleep there tonight and every night you wish."

"Thanks," Fargo said as a man came from the

house. He was tall, well-built, with curly brown hair, his good looks marred by a mean line to his mouth.

"You brought a visitor with you, Magdalena," he said.

"A man who has come to see Señor Rogers. I showed him the way, Señor Kirby," she said, and made no mention of what had happened to her uncle. Fargo wondered why not, but knew he'd keep her confidence.

"I've been sent for," Fargo said to the man. "Name's Fargo . . . Skye Fargo."

Kirby made no effort to conceal the instant displeasure that came to his face. "Ah, yes, the answer to a maiden's prayer," he said, the sneer unmistakable in his voice.

"I try to be." Fargo smiled but brought no change in the man's obvious dislike.

"This way," Kirby said, and led him into the house.

Fargo found himself in a large living room, richly furnished with thick rugs, carved oak tables, and leather-covered chairs and sofas. A man rose from one of the chairs, very tall and straight-backed, silver-haired with a patrician face and light-blue eyes, a man who wore authority without pretension.

"Skye Fargo," Kirby announced, and the silver-haired man stepped forward with an expansive smile.

"I'm Philip Rogers," he said. "Welcome to Rancho Rogers. How about some coffee?"

"I'd like that," Fargo said, and Rogers turned and called over his shoulder to an adjoining room.

"Sit down, please," Philip Rogers said, and Fargo lowered himself onto the leather sofa as an elderly man in a white servant's coat appeared with a tray and two steaming mugs of coffee. Fargo tossed a glance at Kirby and saw the sneer remained on his face.

"You met Alden," Rogers said after a sip of coffee.

"Not really." Fargo smiled.

"Alden Kirby, my ranch manager," Rogers said, and gave the man a nod. He received no response. Rogers sat down across from Fargo, an expansive graciousness in his smile. "Welcome, and thank you for making that long trip," he said.

"You sent a powerful lot of travel money."

"Let me tell you something about myself and this great land we call the Sierras. My family grew up here, before the gold strike. We bred, raised, and sold only the finest of horses. I've kept that tradition. We breed only the best, and I never lack for buyers."

"I saw some of them in the corrals. Damn fine specimens, all right," Fargo agreed.

"There are at least another half-dozen ranchers in the valley, and another few on smaller mountain plots, all Americans. I'm the largest and the wealthiest. No bragging, just the facts of it. There are a number of hardworking trappers and farmers, mostly Americans, many who never made it in the gold rush. Then there is the very sizable population of Mexicans and those of Mexican descent. Some farm, some work at the ranches, some make pottery and sell it," Rogers explained. "But in the past six months we've been plagued by a damn gang of bandits who raid, kill, and steal. Mostly they've been hitting the ranchers like myself. Some six of us have banded together to stop them, but we've had no damn luck at all. That's when I decided to send for you."

"I heard something about these bandits. I happened to meet Magdalena on my way here," Fargo said. "But I don't see where a trailsman fits into this."

"I told you, Mr. Rogers. He's only good for breaking steer trails," Alden Kirby snapped.

"I happen to know that Fargo has trailed more than one killer," Philip Rogers said, his eyes staying on

Fargo, and the big man shrugged. "These bastards hit, run, and disappear. They obviously split up; they have a plan that works and keep getting away with it. I want you to pick up their trails. From what I've heard, you're the one man who might be able to do it."

"A waste of money," Kirby interjected.

"Alden wasn't in favor of my sending for you," Rogers explained with a smile.

"I sort of got that idea," Fargo said blandly.

"I'll nail them. It's just going to take more time," Alden said.

"And that time may be all they need to hit me hard," the rancher said. "They already hit George Dodd hard, robbed him of ten thousand in cash. Ben Dorrance lost a coin collection worth thousands." Philip Rogers suddenly broke off as a figure came into the room.

Fargo rose to take in a young woman. He found himself staring. She had the kind of beauty that demanded it. She was tall, with her father's patrician features, but with long, sleek black hair and eyes of black fire, a very white skin, and sharply etched lips. A pale-pink blouse over a black skirt added to the shimmering exquisiteness of her. He took in a slender, willowy figure with breasts that curved up in a long, lovely line. But she was more than that. Those were only the things of the flesh. He remembered how Magdalena had described her. Disdain was apparent in Isabel Rogers, aristocratic condescension. But there was more than Magdalena saw. Isabel Rogers had an air to her, indeed, but it was an amused challenge, as though she were perpetually daring others to meet her expectations.

She was, he decided, fire and ice.

"Skye Fargo," she said, her eyes fastened on him.

"I've been curious after all the things Father's told me about you."

"My daughter, Isabel," Philip Rogers introduced, and Fargo saw the young woman's eyes stay on him, the challenge in their black depths.

"Stories have a way of being exaggerated." Fargo smiled and saw her eyes move up and down his tall, powerful frame.

"They sure do," Alden Kirby broke in.

Isabel smiled, a dazzling flash that made her lovely face glow with animation. "Alden doesn't approve of Father's sending for you. But you know that already," she said.

"How about you? Do you approve?" Fargo asked.

"I reserved judgment," she said. "Are you going to disappoint me?"

"Probably," Fargo said, and her laugh was low and throaty.

"The answer of a man who believes just the opposite," she observed, and Fargo allowed a smile in return.

Philip Rogers broke in. "What do you say, Fargo? Will you trail these vicious killers for us?"

"It's not what I was expecting," Fargo said. "I expected you wanted me to break a new trail over the mountains for a herd."

"The man means he knows when he's into something he can't handle," Alden Kirby said with a harsh laugh.

"Is that right?" Philip Rogers asked.

"I don't know. It's not my cup of tea, exactly," Fargo said.

"You've trailed many a killer, Fargo." Roger frowned.

"This is a gang of very bad customers," Alden

Kirby interjected. "Fargo's smart enough to back off, especially when he knows I have things in hand."

"Is that so?" Fargo asked mildly.

"Damn right," Kirby snapped. "Maybe you saw some of my guards when you rode in."

"I did. That your doing?" Fargo asked.

"Mr. Rogers told me to secure the ranch. That's the most important thing. Now I just need more time to trail them down," Kirby said, gathering importance with every word. He was an arrogant man whose position as cock-of-the-walk had been impugned when Philip Rogers sent for him, Fargo realized. Alden Kirby wouldn't be mollified or placated. The only way to cut him down was to expose his errors. The man's hostility was plain, and Fargo wondered for a moment if there were perhaps other reasons for it besides his personal conceit.

"Well, Fargo?" Philip Rogers cut in.

"Kirby, here, says he has everything under control," Fargo said. "You're satisfied of that, it seems."

"Indeed, but a trailsman brings special talents. That's why I sent for you," Rogers said.

Fargo let his lips purse as thoughts raced through his mind and he paused to meet Kirby's satisfied smirk. "I don't know. I'd like to think about this," Fargo said. "Sleep on it."

"Yes, you've had a long trip and I'm sure you're still tired. Think about it and we'll talk some more tomorrow," Rogers said. "You've made a hard trip. It'd be a shame to have it wasted."

"I'll see Fargo out, Father," Isabel said.

"Use your charms to convince him to help us," Rogers said, and she smiled as she fell in step beside Fargo. Outside, he saw her eyes go over the Ovaro with expert appreciation.

"A very impressive animal," she said.

"He's special," Fargo said, and saw her fasten him with a thoughtful, sidelong glance, a small smile on her finely etched lips.

"You don't think Alden has things in hand," she mentioned, and he swore inwardly at the sharpness of her as he let his eyes linger on the lovely upward curve of her breasts under the pink blouse.

"I didn't say that," he demurred.

"You didn't have to," Isabel laughed. "But you surprise me, Fargo."

"Why?"

"You don't seem the type who'd turn down a challenge?" she said, her eyes still studying him.

"You're that good a judge of character?" Fargo smiled.

"I have my ways. From inside more than outside."

"Everybody makes a mistake sometime." He shrugged.

"I don't usually," she answered, and he swung onto the Ovaro. He wanted to get away from her sharp, intuitive probing, all of it entirely too accurate. He met her dark eyes as they continued to peer hard at him. Fire and ice, he told himself again, fire and ice. It was a volatile mixture, opposites as intriguing as they were dangerous, as unpredictable as beautiful.

"Sorry to disappoint you," Fargo said as he put the pinto into a canter and hurried away. He took in Alden Kirby's guards as he rode from the ranch and passed under the iron arch. He headed from the plateau into the low hills with the towering mountains of the Sierra Nevada just behind. He scanned the land and saw how easy it would be to strike at the ranches and be back in the thickly forested low hills in minutes.

He rode slowly through the low hills, noting the absence of any real trails and the existence of hundreds of twisting passageways that led to hundreds of small hills. Besides the white fir and the quaking aspen, the hills held profuse growths of blue spruce mixed in with the Sierra junipers. Fargo halted finally at a spot that let him look down and across the low plateau, the Rogers ranch hardly visible now. Philip Rogers had offered him the kind of money a man doesn't turn down, and he had made the long trip here. Besides, nothing so beautiful as Isabel Rogers should be left to fall into the hands of a band of thieving cutthroats.

But Alden Kirby would be a problem. He'd argue on every point, interfere, challenge—anything to assert his authority. He'd make it a contest for Philip Rogers' support, and that would never do. If he stayed, he'd have to cut Kirby down fast and hard, expose his stupidity, shoot holes in the cloak of acceptance he'd managed to wear. It was the only way, Fargo realized as he moved the Ovaro on through the low hills.

He took in the terrain, moving in a long circle as he threaded his way through the Sierra junipers, making mental notes as he rode, letting small details of the land fold themselves into his mind. Finally, he returned to the plateau and stayed inside a long line of blue spruce that grew close to Rancho Rogers.

He walked the pinto in the tree cover and drew as close to the ranch as possible. His lake-blue eyes narrowed as they swept the outer perimeter of the ranch. He picked out most of the guards Alden Kirby had positioned, and he uttered a snort of disgust as he finally turned the horse around and made his way back through the trees.

The day's end eventually drew near, the blue-gray of dusk giving way to a delicate purple, and he rode slowly through the gently rolling hills. He still had plenty of time to wait, his decision already made, and

33

he steered the horse along the narrow road that led to Magdalena's place. Night had fallen when he reached it and saw the lamplight inside the house.

He dismounted and went to the door. Magdalena's eyes widened with surprise and pleasure as she saw him. She rushed to him, her arms circling his neck for an instant. "You've come, Fargo. I was hoping you would."

"Not to stay," he said, and her frown of disappointment was instant. "Tomorrow night, maybe," he said, and she let the frown vanish with a quick smile.

"You can stay for some *arroz con frijoles*? It is all ready and waiting," she said.

"Yes, I can do that," Fargo said.

Magdalena led him into a small kitchen with a round, wooden table in the center. She served a shot glass of tequila and a heaping plate of the steaming rice and sat down opposite him, plainly enjoying the role of hostess. She had changed into a shapeless, gray smocklike gown, yet the heavy, round curves of her breasts refused to be ignored. She chattered brightly with a simple directness. Naturalness was a part of her, and Fargo thought of how she had curled up alongside him during the night.

"You cannot stay tonight. Did you come to tell me that?" she asked.

"No, I came to ask things," Fargo said. "You said nothing at the ranch about how we met or what happened to your uncle. Why not?"

Magdalena's round face darkened at once and she didn't answer for a long moment. "I don't know if you can understand, Fargo," she said finally. "There has been talk that these *bandidos* are made up of my people, a gang of the poor who have decided to attack the rich *americanos*. I am sure this is not so, Fargo. The people here have always lived happily together.

34

My people are poor, but they are honest and hard-working. But there is talk, and Alden Kirby is one who believes this."

"Philip Rogers go along with it?"

"I don't know. I have never heard him say so. But Kirby has some of the other ranchers agreeing with him," Magdalena said. "If I told Alden Kirby what happened to Uncle Pedro, he would only say it was proof. He would say Uncle Pedro recognized the men he saw and had to run for his life."

"Can't rule it out completely, Magdalena," Fargo said, his voice gentle.

"I rule it out. I cannot believe it. Uncle Pedro looked as though he had seen *el diablo* himself and he could only run in shock and terror. But Alden Kirby will believe the other, I know it," she said.

"I understand how you feel," Fargo said, and put a hand alongside her soft cheek. Fear, shame, and pride all whirled inside her, he realized, and he felt sorry for her. "But Kirby, Philip Rogers, they all know about your Uncle Pedro. They know you have lived with him, been raised by him. You can't have him suddenly disappear. You'll have to tell them, like it or not. If you don't, and they hear of his death on their own, it will look worse."

She met his eyes with a long, solemn gaze, and suddenly she was against him, clinging to him, her face buried in his chest. "Of course, you are right," she said. "Thank you for understanding, for helping me again. I will tell them tomorrow. I'll tell them what happened. That's all I know. I can't tell them more."

"It's best that way, for you, especially," Fargo said, and she clung to him a moment longer. She lifted her round face and he felt her lips, warm and soft against his, and then she pulled away.

"We have a saying here: bad things happen to bring

pain; good things happen to help you stand the pain," she said. "You are one of those good things, Fargo."

He patted her soft, full rear as he stepped back. "I'd best be going," he said.

She nodded and walked to the door with him. "Did you find out why Señor Rogers sent for you, Fargo?"

"He wants me to trail those *bandidos*," Fargo said, and saw the surprise come into Magdalena's face.

"Are you going to do it?"

"Tell you tomorrow." He laughed and hurried into the night. She waved as he rode away and he sent the Ovaro down the road and west toward the Rogers ranch.

The moon had swung high in the sky, Fargo noted with satisfaction. The hour had grown late enough. He made his way to the low plateau, then slowed and melted into the line of blue spruce that wandered into the ranch. He halted and swung to the ground as he spotted the first of Alden Kirby's guards along the perimeter of the ranch. He took the lariat in one hand, left the Ovaro in the trees, and moving on steps silent as a lynx in snow, he circled behind the first of the guards.

The man lounged against a tree, his rifle leaning alongside him. It was plain that he was listening only for the sound of a pack of horses, and Fargo drew the big Colt as he crept closer to the man. He turned the gun in his hand so that he gripped it by the barrel. When he reached the tree, he half-rose, the guard still completely unaware of him, and brought the butt of the revolver down on the man's head. He stepped from behind the tree and caught the guard before he toppled sideways, and lowered him silently to the ground. He used the lariat next, bound the man, and gagged him with his own kerchief.

He turned, crept back into the trees, and made his

way to where Kirby's second sentry waited. This one was no more alert than the first, Fargo noted as once again he circled, came up behind the man, and brought the butt of the Colt down on his head. When he was finished binding the man, he crept toward the third sentry he had observed not far from one of the stables. He could have left the third, but he decided to emphasize his point.

The guard was more in the open, standing against the fence that bordered the stables. Fargo waited, measured distances, and crossed the open space at a crouching run. The gun crashed down on the man before he had a chance to turn, and Fargo not only bound and gagged him but tied him to the fence. There were others, at least three more on the back part of the outer perimeter of the ranch, but he'd let them stay untouched. They'd not bother him any. Nor anyone else, he grunted wryly as he returned to the Ovaro and led the horse through the trees. He halted where the spruce ended, the main house a dozen yards away, standing dark and still.

He dropped to one knee, waited for the moon to vanish behind a passing cloud, and moved quickly, the Ovaro at his heels. He was at the rear of the house when the pale light reappeared. He found the back door quickly, turned the knob, and heard the latch click open. Inside the house, he saw a dim night lamp giving just enough light for him to find his way past the kitchen, a den, and the large living room. He paused, saw a wide corridor stretch out beyond the living room with another dim night lamp hanging from one wall. He saw closed doors on both sides of the wide corridor as he made his way along the carpeted floor.

He halted at the first door. His big hand closed around the doorknob and turned the knob carefully.

He peered into a room where enough moonlight streamed through the window to let him see a guest room with a single bed to one side.

He closed the first door and stepped to the one across the corridor. Again, he opened the door just wide enough to let him peer in. He heard the deep, heavy sound of a man's breathing and saw a large room, a four-poster bed against one side. He spotted the figure inside the big bed. Obviously the master bedroom, with Philip Rogers hard asleep inside it.

Fargo closed the door and went on to the next one. It turned out to be another guest room. The fourth closed door across the corridor opened to reveal another guest room.

Only one door remained at the far end of the corridor, and Fargo hurried to it. He paused and knew he had found the room he sought even before he opened the door. The distinctive odor of cologne and powder seeped from the room, subtly provocative. He opened the door and the delicately intriguing odor swirled over him. He stepped into a room filled with deep cushions and colors that were bold even in the dim moonlight—no fussy frills, yet boldly feminine, just like its occupant.

He smiled as he moved toward the sleeping form in the double bed. He halted when he reached the bedside: Isabel was sound asleep, a light sheet covering her from the waist down. She wore a white silk nightgown and lay on her side, the lovely curve of one breast dipping from the neck of the gown, thin straps revealing rounded, broad shoulders, her hair a black halo against the pillow.

He leaned forward and closed one hand over her mouth. Her eyes snapped open. "Quiet," he whispered. "Nobody's going to hurt you." She blinked up at him and he saw recognition come into her eyes and drew his hand away. She sat up at once and pulled the sheet up with one hand.

"You," she said, frowning. "What are you doing here?"

"Get some clothes on. We're going on a little trip."

"Are you mad? I'm not going anywhere," Isabel Rogers said, and he saw her eyes narrow at him. "Maybe you're not even Skye Fargo. Maybe you're a damn imposter," she hissed.

"I'm Fargo," he said. "Now get dressed. I haven't time to explain."

"You get out of here," Isabel snapped, and he saw her mouth drop open to scream. His fist shot out, a quick, glancing blow that snapped up on the point of her chin. Isabel fell back on the bed, unconscious.

He swore to himself as he glanced about, saw a shirt and a pair of Levi's, and stuffed both into his belt. He lifted Isabel's limp form, slung her over his shoulder, and hurried from the room. He made his way down the corridor, the soft warmth of her pressed against him, and he left by the rear door. Outside, he draped Isabel across the saddle on her stomach and swung onto the Ovaro himself. He walked the horse across the open space and into the line of spruce, keeping the horse at a walk through the trees. Not hurrying, he held her in place with one hand on her rear. Soft firmness, tight and modest, he made note idly. It fitted the rest of her long, slender shape.

Fargo left the ranch and rode across the low plateau still in tree cover. He was in the low hills when he felt Isabel come awake. He halted, dismounted, and pulled her to the ground. He held her as she steadied herself for a moment, blinking up at him, the long curves of her tight against the clinging silk of the nightgown. She gathered herself in seconds and he saw her right arm move. His hand was up and blocked the slap she aimed at him.

"Bastard," she hissed.

"Relax, honey," he said. "Nothing's going to happen to you." He pulled the Levi's and shirt from his belt and tossed them at her. "Here, put these on."

She caught the clothes, her black eyes still boring into him. "Am I supposed to say thank you?" she speared icily.

"You could," Fargo said calmly. "I didn't have to bring them."

"A moment of weakness or gallantry?" she sniffed.

"Maybe they're the same thing," he said, and she spun on her heel and strode behind a tree.

He was in the saddle when she returned, the ice still in her lovely, patrician face.

"There's a good spot to bed down a hundred yards or so on," Fargo said.

"I'll walk," she snapped.

"Suit yourself," he returned, and moved forward on the pinto. He kept the horse at a walk and watched her trudging after him. He halted at a small arbor of spruce and white fir. He dismounted and met her glare as she faced him, hands on her hips.

"Maybe you'd like to tell me what this is all about? Why did you snatch me from my bedroom and bring me here?" she asked, anger in her lovely face.

"I'm making a point," Fargo said calmly, and saw her eyebrows lift.

"Making a point?"

"Loud and clear," he said. "You could be in the hands of those *bandidos* now. They wouldn't be at all nice to you."

Her frown stayed as her black eyes bored into him.

"I'm beginning to understand," Isabel Rogers said slowly. "I guess you did make your point."

"I'd say so," Fargo answered dryly.

"But you didn't have to go this far. You enjoyed taking me off in my nightgown like some caveman," she accused.

"Had to." He shrugged.

"Rubbish. You made your way into my room. That would have been enough," Isabel muttered.

"No. Kirby would have weaseled. He'd claim that I got in to the house, but I'd never have been able to get out with you. You know that's what he'd say. But he can't now."

Her half-shrug was an admission, but the glower stayed in her face. "You didn't have to hit me," she muttered.

"Your fault. You were going to scream," he said, and pulled an extra blanket from behind his saddle roll. He tossed it on the ground and let it spread out. "Settle down. We've a few hours till morning," he said, and she didn't move. "You want to change back into your nightgown again?" he slid at her.

"You'd like that, wouldn't you?" Isabel snapped.

"Just want you to be comfortable, honey," he said.

She uttered a wry snort as he pulled off his shirt, undressed down to his Levi's, and stretched out at one side of the blanket. She didn't hide the frank appreciation in her eyes as she took in his muscled symmetry. She lowered herself to the other side of the blanket and he saw the smile slide across her face, a cool smugness in it.

"I was right," she murmured.

"About what?"

"About you. You're not the kind to turn down a challenge."

"Feel better now?" he asked.

"Definitely," she said. "It's good to know your instincts are always right."

"Get some sleep," he growled, and refused to let her know he understood her triumph.

# 3

He let the morning sun come fully over the Sierras before he woke her and offered his canteen to freshen up. When she finished, he swung onto the pinto. "It's a long way back to the ranch. Still want to walk?" Fargo asked mildly.

"I'll ride," Isabel said, and he pulled her onto the saddle in front of him. She rode well, slender body swaying easily in rhythm with the horse, her small, tight rear touching against him. She cast a glance back at him, the cool, appraising smile of her lips. "You're something different," Isabel Rogers remarked.

"Whatever that means," Fargo said.

"I'm not sure yet," she said as they reached the edge of the plateau. "You'll have Alden as an enemy when he learns about this," she mentioned. "It'll be a direct slap in his face."

"Sometimes you make friends. Sometimes you make enemies," Fargo said unconcernedly, and drew a tiny, low laugh from Isabel.

"A practical philosophy," she said.

He put the pinto into a canter and she leaned back against his chest. Her slender body possessed its own wiry strength. He passed under the wrought-iron arch and the houses of the ranch came into view. He saw the cluster of figures in front of the main house as he drew closer, agitated, gesticulating, the sunlight catching Philip Rogers' silver hair.

Fargo picked out Alden Kirby and two other men, but Rogers was the first to see him approach with Isabel.

"My God," Philip Rogers shouted as he ran forward and Fargo brought the horse to a halt. "You found her. Thank God you found her," Rogers said as Isabel slid to the ground and he caught her in his arms and held her tight. Finally he released his daughter and turned to Fargo. "We found the three guards first, and when I realized Isabel was missing, I knew they'd taken her. How did you find her, Fargo?"

Fargo exchanged a glance with Isabel and let her reply. "He didn't find me, Father. He took me," she said evenly.

Fargo dismounted as Philip Rogers stared at his daughter, turned his eyes slowly to Fargo, and then back to her as a frown of uncomprehension furrowed his brow.

"What are you saying, Isabel?" Rogers murmured.

"He came in the night, took care of those three guards, got into the house, and came to my room and carried me off," she said.

Rogers pulled his eyes from Isabel to stare at Fargo. "Is that right?" he demanded.

"Every word of it," Fargo said almost cheerfully.

"I don't understand. Why, for God's sake? What's the meaning of this?" Philip Rogers shot back, anger coming into his voice.

"The meaning is, if I got in, so could those bandits. Only your three guards would be dead and Isabel wouldn't be standing here now," Fargo said calmly, and glanced at Alden Kirby, to see the man's face grow red.

"This is a damn cheap trick," Kirby snapped.

"This is an object lesson, mister," Fargo snapped back. "Loud and clear."

Alden Kirby's lips twitched as he looked at Philip Rogers, and Fargo saw Rogers slowly nod, his eyes still on the big man in front of him. "An object lesson," he repeated slowly. "Yes, I'm afraid it certainly is that."

"Goddamn, Philip, you're not going to pay attention to this stunt, are you?" Kirby protested.

"I'm sorry, Alden, but this stunt showed that the ranch certainly wasn't secure," Rogers said.

"Dammit, he got lucky," Kirby returned.

Fargo's laugh was a harsh sound. "I think you believe that, Kirby. That's the sad part."

Alden Kirby stepped forward, his fists clenched. "I ought to smash your damn face in," he threatened.

"I'd think real carefully about that," Fargo said calmly.

Philip Rogers stepped forward. "Calm down, Alden. We can't let bruised feelings get in the way of fact. The safety of the ranch is the important thing. Fargo's object lesson was a hard one, but all too effective, I'm afraid," Rogers said, and turned to Fargo. "I take it you've some ideas on properly protecting the ranch."

"You can't secure a place this big. The house is the important thing, isn't it?" Fargo said.

"That's right." Rogers nodded.

"Then we bring your guards in closer. They were out too far and too far away from one another. Hell, a buffalo could've sneaked through," Fargo said. "Call everybody together and I'll position them."

Rogers turned to Kirby, but the man was already striding away, anger rising from him in almost visible waves. "Alden's pride has been hurt. He'll get over it," Rogers said, and fastened Fargo with a piercing stare. "I'm not sure I approve of your methods, Fargo, effective as they were. Carrying Isabel off that way must have been a terrible experience for her."

"It could've been worse," Fargo reminded the man, and Philip Rogers let a grim smile come to his lips.

"You ever question yourself, Fargo?" he asked.

"As little as possible," Fargo said, and turned with Rogers to see Alden Kirby returning with the men, including the three he had tied up, he noted. Kirby walked away as the men halted in front of Rogers.

"This is Skye Fargo," Rogers introduced. "He's going to take charge of securing the ranch." He stood back as Fargo moved among the men and began to position each guard in a circle between the main house and the outlying barns, stables, and corrals. He found unobtrusive spots for each and set up four-hour rotating shifts. It took time before he was satisfied, and when he finished, the sun was well past the noon hour. "Visit the other ranchers with me, Fargo. I know they'll want to meet you, and you ought to have a look at their places, anyway," Rogers said. "But first I want to have a talk with Alden."

"Soothing ruffled feathers?" Fargo commented.

"Yes, he's been a fine ranch manager. I don't want to lose him," Rogers said, and beckoned to Isabel. "Come along. You know Alden will listen to you." The young woman nodded and fell into step beside her father as Philip Rogers made his way to Alden Kirby's quarters, a small building between the barn and the bunkhouse.

Fargo turned away and relaxed against the front of the main house, and he saw Magdalena appear with a cart of wash.

"Hello, *mi amigo*." She smiled warmly.

"You talk to Philip Rogers yet?" he asked.

"No, he has been so busy with you. But I will tell

him before the day ends, I promise," she said, and he patted her shoulder as she went past.

Philip Rogers returned a few minutes later, alone, and paused at Fargo. "I'll get my horse," he said.

"Isabel still placating him?" Fargo smiled.

"She'll do a better job than I will," Rogers said, and hurried into the stable. He returned on a beautiful dark-gray mount with the conformation and fire that shouted fine breeding.

They rode west, the first stop a spread owned by a man named Matt Stove. Two of the other ranchers were there, Ben Dorrance and George Dodd. Stove's spread wasn't as large as Philip Rogers', but it was plenty big by ordinary standards. He specialized in standardbreds. The three ranchers were genuinely glad to see Fargo.

"Call on us if we can help. You're doing a favor for us all if you can track down these bastards," Matt Stover told him as he left with Philip Rogers.

Fargo scanned the terrain as they rode. Philip took him to the other spreads, some smaller, all well-tended, all impressive. Their owners were all wealthy men, some retired to enjoy their wealth. The last stop was the smallest outfit, on the way back toward Rancho Rogers. There he met Hod and Dora Carter.

There was only one way onto their land, Fargo noted, a cut through a circle of high rock. Carter had three sentries at the entranceway. He and his wife, a pleasant-faced, thin woman, served coffee and Hod Carter spoke about his fears. "Dora used to complain how we were surrounded by rock formations. Now she's happy for it," the man said. "I never was a rancher. Everyone knows I've one of the finest rare-gem collections in California. But we actually feel safer here than most of the others."

"You might be," Fargo said as he scanned the

smooth rock sides that surrounded the land. When he left with Rogers, they returned to the Rogers ranch.

Isabel waited outside, her willowy form in a tight-fitting black riding outfit. She stepped forward as Rogers stabled his horse.

"Have you come back with any ideas?" she asked Fargo.

"I'm considering some," he said.

"Will you stay for dinner?"

"Sorry, not tonight," he demurred.

"Magdalena?" Isabel smiled, and Fargo knew he hadn't been able to halt the flash of surprise that caught at him.

"A good guess or intuition?" he asked.

She offered a smile of cool amusement. "A little of each. You'd said you met her before arriving here. The rest was simple," she said. "And rather amusing."

"Amusing?"

"Perhaps I'll answer that another time," she said, and strolled into the house in that walk that was both contained and sensuous.

Fargo waited for Philip Rogers to return before swinging the horse in a circle. "See you tomorrow, sometime," he told the man.

"I understand," Rogers said.

Fargo put the pinto into a slow trot and rode from the ranch. He halted in the low hills, his eyes sweeping the terrain as thoughts tumbled through his mind, some to discard, others to hold in abeyance.

When darkness rolled down from the high Sierras, he turned the horse east and rode until he reached Magdalena's place. He could smell the stew before he dismounted.

She had a glass of tequila waiting for him with the rim well salted. She wore a loose, full blouse with a low neck over a black skirt. "It is good to make dinner for you, Fargo," she said.

"It's good to be here. Damn tasty, too," he said as he sampled the stew.

"I spoke to Señor Rogers just before I left for the day. I told him about Uncle Pedro and how you almost saved him," she said. "Isabel was there, too."

"He say anything?"

"He thanked me for telling him," Magdalena answered, "and I told him it was everything I knew."

"That's good, Magdalena," Fargo said. "It's better to have come from you."

Her hand came over his. "You have been so good, so caring. I wish I could help you catch those who killed Pedro."

"Maybe you will. Funny things happen."

"I will pray for it. Meanwhile, my home is yours," she said, and paused. "I am yours," she added very softly.

He cupped her chin in one hand. "I don't take that kind of thanks, Magdalena," he said. "Now, let's finish this delicious stew."

She smiled and returned to the meal. After he downed the last of it with the tequila, he helped her carry the clay plates into the kitchen.

She turned to him, her deep breasts pressed hard against the blouse. "The room is yours. Sleep well," she said as she closed the front door and blew out the lamp.

He found a candle burning in the adjoining room, undressed, and stretched out on the low mattress-bed. He lay with his hands behind his head and the question that danced in his mind found a quick answer as Magdalena came into the room. She wore the knee-length cotton nightgown and she curled up alongside him as she had the night before. But this time he felt her hands reach up to his chest. Her round face followed, pressed against his muscled nakedness, and he felt her lips touch his pectorals, a soft, damp touch.

"I do not come for thanking," Magdalena murmured. "I come for wanting."

He reached down and lifted her face. Her eyes were black pools caught by the flickering candlelight. He leaned down, pressed his lips on hers, and felt the softness respond at once. "You sure?" he asked.

She opened her lips and he felt her tongue push forward, caress his mouth, probe deeply, draw back, and stay against his. "Does this answer you, Fargo?" she whispered.

"I'd say so," he replied, and Magdalena pushed away and flung the nightgown from her in a quick, joyous motion. He took in the large, deep breasts, each tipped by a large dark-red nipple on a circle of matching tone. Her rib cage was wide, hips to match, a convex little belly, and below it, a wild, unruly black nap. She had a fleshy body, but youth gave it firmness and earthy sensuousness, even to her thighs, which seemed not so much chunky as invitingly soft.

Her deep breasts flattened against his chest, pillows of warmth that made his own skin tingle. He fell back, brought her with him, and smothered his face into the twin mounds of softness. His mouth found one dark-red tip to pull upon, to draw in as much as possible.

"Oh God . . ." Magdalena cried out as she brought the other full mound to his lips. She was all softness and eagerness, pushing, rubbing, pressing herself up against his exploring hands. He caressed the little belly and felt the sexy roundness of it.

She screamed as he moved down into the wild triangle where little ends of wiry black hair fell against her thighs. Her hand came down, found him, and again she cried out, this time a scream of delight. "Ah, yes, yes . . . *qué grande* . . . oh, oh," she murmured.

He turned and pushed his throbbing erectness against the soft belly and again Magdalena screamed. Her hands clutched at his back and he felt the dampness of her thighs as they fell open and clasped themselves against his ribs. "Oh, Fargo, Fargo . . . please, oh yes, yes . . . *por favor*," she gasped and he felt her push up against him. She twisted, turned, arched her body upward, and he felt the wetness of her wanting against his groin. "*Cógeme*," she demanded. "Take me. For you, Fargo, for you, *mi amigo*." She pushed upward again against him, and he let himself slide into her—wide wetness, overwhelming warmth, inner softness to match outer flesh.

"Aaaaagh," Magdalena groaned, suddenly a deep sound, and then again, ecstasy given voice from the depths of the body. She seized his head and pulled his face into her deep, full breasts, which now swayed and bounced, closed around him with suffocating sweetness. She thrust upward with him, all earthly, overwhelming wanting. Her full, soft thighs clamped against him, the concave little belly damp, adhering to his own flesh, bodies welding together, flesh exploding in turbulent ecstasy.

Magdalena's cry was a surging groan that seemed to convulse her firm-fleshed body as it trembled, shook, vibrated, and finally fell back onto the bed with him. Soft moaning sounds came from her, joy and despair mixed together. She held his face against her breasts. He stayed, let his lips caress one dark-red tip until she went limp and a deep sigh escaped her lips. "*Maravilloso*," she breathed. "We sleep now, you and I."

"Yes, we sleep now," he said, and she turned on her side, pressed against him, and once again, little-girl fashion, slept with the peace of the unpretending.

He held her and enjoyed the round softness of her until he slipped off to sleep himself.

He woke with the dawn, swung from the bed, washed and dressed, and then heard Magdalena stir and rise. She was dressed when he returned from the rear of the house with the Ovaro, and he helped her hitch her cart. "Maybe we oughtn't to arrive at the Rogers place together. Tongues have a way of wagging," he said, and she nodded in understanding.

"We can ride part of the way together," she said, and he swung in alongside the cart. She drove west, climbed a low hill, and halted as Fargo reined to a stop. He peered down at a row of figures moving single-file below. He counted a dozen, each clothed in a brown robe and brown hood, a white cincture around each figure's waist.

"Some of the friars from the mission with Father Junípero," Magdalena said.

The wide and deep hoods obscured their faces. He could see nothing but brown-cloaked figures. "How do you know which one's Father Junípero?" he asked.

"He is the first in line and wears the heavy cross around his neck."

"Sorry, I'm not much on friars," Fargo said, and took note of the heavy agate cross against the chest of the first figure.

"Come, I will introduce you to him. I'm sure he has heard about you by now. All news finds its way to the mission," Magdalena said. She drove down to the path and halted in front of the line of brown-robed figures. The monks had been chanting as they walked, and the murmur of their voices came to a halt as the first figure lifted his head to peer forward.

"Magdalena, good morning," the man said.

"Good morning, Father," she said. "This is Skye

Fargo, the man Señor Rogers has called in to track down the *bandidos*."

"Ah, yes, I have heard of your arrival," the priest said as he turned to Fargo. His hood moved back enough for Fargo to see a lined, lean face with a thin mouth, a straight nose, and surprisingly bright-blue eyes. It was a face that, in other surroundings, might be called hard, but was ascetic and austere inside the hooded robe. "Bless you," Father Junípero said. "These are hard times indeed."

Magdalena tells me you've had your store of troubles," Fargo said.

"Yes, terrible, terrible things. She has told you the details?"

"No," Fargo said.

Father Junípero turned to Magdalena. "Word has come to me about Pedro. I expected you would be at the chapel for special prayers, my dear," he said.

"I am coming this afternoon, Father," she said.

Father Junípero turned to Fargo again. "Maybe you will visit the mission with Magdalena this afternoon. We can talk more, then," he said.

"Yes, I'd like that," Fargo said.

Father Junípcro smiled, nodded, and moved on, the brown hood falling forward. The friars followed and Fargo could only glimpse the dim outlines of their faces inside the hoods as each dipped his head as he passed. Their murmured chanting began again as they shuffled on, a brown line that echoed distant centuries.

"Where are they going?" Fargo asked Magdalena.

"Probably to gather greens and mushrooms for the evening meal," she said. "I must get to the ranch, Fargo. I'll be back at my house by four."

"I'll be there," Fargo said, and watched her drive on. He rode north and made a long, slow circle into the low hills. He looked forward to a visit to the mission. If everything found its way to the mission, as Magdalena had said, perhaps he could enlist the good friars to listen carefully to anything their parishioners might say. It was worth trying, he mused as his long circle took him to the edge of Hod and Dora Carter's place. He halted to scan the rocks around the spread and again concluded it was the most secure of all the ranches. He glimpsed one of the guards at the pathway down to the house as he rode on, his eyes again sweeping the terrain that bordered the great Sierra Nevada Range. He followed a long stand of piñon pine that led back toward the Rogers ranch, and when he rode through the iron arch, the sun had just passed the noon hour.

He saw Philip Rogers with Alden Kirby and two hands at a section of fencing that had come loose. As he drew to a halt at the main house, Isabel came out. Her onyx hair gleamed in the sun against a pure white, tailored blouse with tan riding britches below. She surveyed him as he dismounted and he saw the cool amusement in her face.

"Enjoy yourself last night?" she slid at him.

"A good meal and pleasant company are always enjoyable," Fargo said, his face impassive.

She let a coolly chiding smile touch her lips. "How gentlemanly," she said.

"Thank you," he tossed back.

She clung to the chiding smile. "Not at all. I'm always amused at how men are invariably attracted to the unsubtle," she said.

"I'm always amused at how women who can't be honest with themselves put down those who are," Fargo remarked.

The black eyes flared for an instant, but her father came from the fence and Isabel swallowed her reply.

"Good to see you, Fargo. Magdalena told us how

you tried to save her uncle," Rogers said. "Terrible, terrible. But obviously he was killed for whatever he saw. Alden views it as further proof of his thinking."

"Which is that the gang is made up of Mexican peasants out to rob the rich Americans and anyone else who has anything," Fargo said.

"You don't accept that?" Rogers asked.

Fargo thought for a moment. "I don't accept it. I don't toss it away, either. Anything's possible."

Philip Rogers smiled. "Fair enough," he said. "You've formed any ideas of your own yet?"

"I'm still nosing around," Fargo said, and Philip nodded as he walked into the house. The Trailsman had begun to walk the pinto on when Isabel's voice reached out.

"You were lying," she said matter-of-factly.

"Why do you say that?" Fargo queried.

The small smile stayed on her finely etched lips. "You wouldn't take this long without some ideas of your own," she returned.

He felt his lips tighten as he silently swore at her sharpness. "Nothing with enough shape to suit me," he said.

"You're still lying," she persisted, and he shot her a glare. But she'd continue to persist and prod, he knew, a combination of her own acuity and her regal attitude that said she had a right to know. Perhaps he was wrong in holding back," he decided. He'd find out how she'd react.

"They're not wild raids," he said. "They have a way to hit, run, and disappear. That means they know the territory. It also means they're led by somebody who can come and go in the region."

"That could fit any of the peasants Alden thinks are behind it."

"It could," Fargo agreed. "And it could also fit any

55

of the ranch managers, including Kirby." He saw the shock pass through her patrician face.

"You can't really believe Alden could be mixed up in this," she protested.

"I don't eliminate anybody for now," he said. "Fact is, I lean toward somebody on the inside someplace, somebody in a position to hear, see, and pick his targets."

"To include Alden in that is preposterous," Isabel snapped angrily.

"You're awfully defensive about Alden Kirby," Fargo remarked casually. "Something personal maybe?"

Her black eyes narrowed. "You can't mean that," she snapped. He met her glare and shrugged, the gesture noncommittal. "You can't possibly think that I'd be involved with Alden," Isabel said, incredulous anger in her tone.

He made a wry sound. "No, not really," he said, and her eyes stayed narrowed but he saw the new question ask itself. He smiled. "You couldn't be," he said.

"Meaning exactly what?" she questioned.

"Meaning you couldn't go for any man you can lead around by the nose," Fargo said. "You'd need somebody who'd tell you where to head in, somebody you'd have to look up to instead of down at."

"My, my. Now you're an expert on the kind of man I'd like," she said.

"I didn't say like. I said need." He grinned and swung onto the Ovaro.

"I can get around easily. I know everyone and what they have in their homes. Maybe I'm the bandit leader," she said, sarcasm draped in each word.

His face stayed expressionless. "Maybe," he said, and turned the horse.

"Go to hell," he heard her say as he rode away.

She couldn't see the smile on his lips, he knew as he rode north through the low hills and climbed into the baseline of the towering Sierras.

After a few hours he halted and realized he was only wasting time. It'd be easy for the raiders to flee into the mountains and hide their loot. One man could do it while the others faded away. There were countless caves to use. Yet it had taken him almost two hours to reach the mountains. Would they risk the time to go that distance? he wondered, his eyes narrowed in thought as he turned the pinto back through the low hills. The longer even one man ran, the more chance he risked of his trail being picked up.

His eyes still narrowed, Fargo set aside the mountains as their refuge. They had to have someplace closer, he decided. Their operation was based on quickness—a fast raid, a strike for a certain object, and a fast disappearance. Closer, he muttered, someplace closer to where they came from. He let thoughts continue to sift through his mind as he rode, and when he finally reached the Rogers ranch, he saw Isabel removing a lunge lead from one of the stallions in the nearest corral.

She came forward, gathering up the long line as she did, and gracefully eased herself between the fence posts to halt in front of him. "I told Father about your ideas that maybe someone from one of the ranches was involved," she said, a challenge in her eyes.

"I expected you would," Fargo said calmly, and saw her mouth tighten.

"Any more wild ideas?"

"I'm going to visit the mission. Maybe I can get the good friars to tell me anything they might hear or see. Little pieces help fill a puzzle," he said. "You go to church at the mission, too?"

"No," Isabel said. "Almost none of the ranchers in

the plateau does and very few Americans in the area. We go to Saint Mary's in High River, even though it's a good hour's ride each way."

"Some special reason?" Fargo inquired.

"I'd say we all like the formality of Saint Mary's, a proper church, not a mission church. We all support the church. It's run by the Jesuits, who operate a school in their best educational tradition," Isabel said somewhat loftily.

"You're saying it's the rich man's church," Fargo remarked.

"It's been called that," she conceded. "It is a wealthy church. It is also a beautiful church, full of the spiritual and intellectual that only the Jesuits can bring. Father Malachy is the pastor."

"Maybe I'll visit sometime with you," Fargo said, and drew a nod with a touch of surprise in it. "Meanwhile, it's the good friars," he finished, and moved the pinto on. He felt her eyes staying on him as he rode away and took a low hillside to cross to Magdalena's place.

She was waiting for him beside the brown mare, which wore a Mexican saddle with the low cantle and *tapaderos*.

"I was about to go myself," she said.

"Sorry. Time got away from me," he apologized, and rode beside her as she headed northeast, across a low hill and down a slope studded with piñon pine and a network of narrow footpaths, some worn dry.

"The trails the friars have made over the centuries," Magdalena said. The land flattened and the mission came into sight—a tall, arched bell tower in the center with a wooden cross at the top. Low walls spread out on both sides of the center entranceway, and higher ones made up the sides and rear of the mission that formed an inside courtyard. Long, narrow buildings with clay-tiled roofs bisected the courtyard, everything built of stone washed white by centuries of sun. The mission architecture echoed the spirit of worship, but in a simple, unpretentious way that offered welcome while exuding an air of cloistered privacy. A shallow hill rose up behind the rear of the mission and Fargo saw the rows of simple crosses planted in the ground.

A length of pine attached to the side of the outer wall served as a hitching post, and Fargo dismounted beside Magdalena, then strode after her as she went through the low, arched doorway. Wall lamps and candles lighted the dim interior of stone walls and long, mazelike corridors that drifted into murky darkness. But the wide doorway in front of him revealed the well-lighted chapel made up of long, backless wooden benches. A stone altar with a plain wood tabernacle and two thin candles in wooden candlesticks were the only objects on the altar. A simple wood cross hung on the blank wall behind.

Magdalena halted at the entrance of the chapel as a robed figure appeared, hood halfway back, and Fargo saw Father Junípero's long, lined, ascetic countenance. The priest halted, put a hand atop Magdalena's head, and his smile was benevolent. "Go into the chapel, my child. Kneel and say your prayers. The brothers have already remembered Pedro at their services," he said, and Magdalena moved past the benches of the chapel. Father Junípero turned to Fargo. "Come, we can talk over here," he said, and stepped to the far wall of one of the long corridors. "It was good of you to come with Magdalena," he said.

"You were going to tell me about the troubles you've had."

"You did not come just to hear that, my son," Father Junípero smiled.

"No," Fargo admitted. "But I'd like to hear about them."

"The terrible tragedy happened six months ago. I arrived here at the mission on one of my regular pilgrimages. Father Antonio was here with the brothers, then. But when I arrived, I found more than half the brothers dead, the rest near death, and Father Antonio barely alive. All alone, I was in a state of shock," Father Junípero said.

"Naturally," Fargo said.

"I managed to get Father Antonio to talk. Brother Julio, the mission cook, made a tragic mistake. When he was gathering mushrooms, a staple of the friars' diet, he mistook the deadly poisonous panther amanita for the edible blusher amanita. It's not a hard thing to do, even for an expert such as Brother Julio was. They were all in the last stages of death by poison. I kept Father Antonio alive for only another day. Those still left died within days."

"God, what a story. You get the people from the villages to help bury everyone?" Fargo asked.

"No. Even in times of tragedy, the Lord provides a way. I was unaware of it, but a dozen new brothers were due at the mission. They arrived the day after the last death. Together, we buried everyone and stayed in mourning for a month after. Since then, another four friars have joined us."

"And you've carried on," Fargo said.

"It is our mission to carry on," Father Junípero said. "For centuries, the Franciscan friars have carried on in the face of tragedy. And now you have something to tell me, my son?"

"I want your help. Magdalena tells me that those who come here to worship talk freely of lots of things. I want the friars to listen carefully to everything they hear. Maybe they'll hear some little thing that might be important. They could maybe make notes and give them to you," Fargo said.

"That can be done. Our parishioners talk of their fears, their jobs, their problems. We will just listen a little more carefully," the priest said.

"I'll check in to find out what you've heard. You'll be the extra ears I need," Fargo said.

Father Junípero nodded and turned as a row of hodded brown-clad figures appeared and moved toward the chapel. He stepped forward when they reached the entranceway, and gestured to the first hooded friar. "This is Brother Martín, Fargo," he introduced, and Fargo glimpsed a round face inside the hood. "Brother Leonardo," the priest said of the next figure, and Fargo managed a glimpse of a long-nosed face inside the hood. A Brother Alfonso was next, followed by a Brother Tomás, Brother Fernando, and Brother Mateo. Fargo introduced each friar and each hooded face nodded respectfully.

"You can count on everyone's help, Fargo," the priest said as the friars filed into the chapel and Magdalena came out. Her lips were tight and a furrow creased her brow, Fargo noted. He watched the brown-robed figures kneel in between the benches and turned to follow Father Junípero and Magdalena as they walked from the building.

"Vespers," the priest said as they stepped outside.

Fargo's eyes swept the mission courtyards, and a frown touched his brow as he saw the line of horses tethered along one rear wall, all saddle mounts, some definitely quarter-horses, others strong-legged mixed bloods. "They yours?" he asked Father Junípero.

"One of the ways the friars raise money. There are always things one must pay for, things they cannot make or raise for themselves. The Church expects its sons and daughters to help themselves. Some orders make brandy and sell it, some wine, some sell their skills as scribes, some run schools. All find a way. The friars sell horses to the ordinary people, those who cannot afford the expensive stock the big ranchers breed. With what little they make and the food the countryside provides, they can stay self-suffient."

"When should I come visiting?" Fargo asked.

"People will come to pray every evening. Come visit in a few days," the priest said, and Fargo nodded, swung onto the Ovaro and waited for Magdalena to mount the brown mare.

They rode from the mission in silence as the night settled over the land. When they reached her place, she went inside while he unsaddled the horses. When he returned to the house, she was on the bed in the knee-length nightgown. He undressed and slid beside her as the long candle flickered. Her arms came around his neck, the softness of the pillowy breasts against his chest.

"I am afraid, Fargo. Suddenly I am afraid," she murmured.

"I thought you'd feel better after visiting the chapel," he said.

"I did. I prayed for Uncle Pedro's soul, and now suddenly I am afraid," she said. "It is as though it was all wasted."

He held her tight. "You're just upset. It's just all catching up to you."

"Maybe, but suddenly, in the chapel, I was afraid, when I should not have been afraid. I had the feeling of death and that the friars could not protect me, not any of us," Magdalena said. "Hold me, love me, Fargo. Maybe you are the only strength here now." She pushed herself out of the nightgown and all her inner turmoil exploded in the refuge that was the senses, the flesh made surrogate for the spirit. Her tongue plumbed deeply into his mouth, her fleshy thighs opening for him, clamping down over him, her breasts smothering his face. Deep, quick groaning sounds came from her as he let her pleasure herself atop him. His hands clasped around her full buttocks helped her pump up and down atop him with desperate wanting. Magdalena cried out and he felt the dampness of her against him as she strained and wanted and urged herself on. He felt his own ecstasy spiraling upward, and Magdalena twisted herself over him, pressed her thighs tighter, and squeezed against his throbbing maleness.

His hands were on her buttocks when her groan erupted, and he let himself explode with her. She fell forward over him as she thrust violently against him, brought her deep breasts onto his face, smothering, pressing, encompassing, as though she could make her flesh his, her senses his own, her flesh melding through his until finally, with another groan, she lay still over him, unmoving, clinging. At last she fell to his side, her breasts heaving with deep breaths. He let her gather herself before he drew her to him. She slept against him in moments, a creature fashioned of the unsubtle satisfactions of the body, her armor against the fears of the mind and spirit.

The candle flickered out and he slept with her breast against his face.

# 4

He rose when morning came, and was washed and dressed when Magdalena woke. "You'll be back tonight?" she asked from the bed.

"Can't say. I'll try."

"Maybe I will see you at the ranch later," she said, and he waved back as he left the house, went to the rear, saddled the Ovaro, and hurried away.

He had decided on an early-morning visit to each ranch. Perhaps a waste of time, but then perhaps not. Little things turned into big leads. Attention to details, those things others overlooked. It was sometimes the only way. He'd decided to start with the Rogers ranch, and he was more than halfway there when he saw a lone horseman galloping toward him and recognized one of Philip Rogers' ranch hands.

The man skidded to a halt, his face red from hard riding. "They want you at the ranch right away. Miss Rogers said you'd be at Magdalena Santas' place," he said.

Fargo nodded and put the Ovaro into a full gallop and held it there until he reached the ranch.

Isabel and her father were outside the house as he rode to a halt, Philip Rogers grim-faced. "They hit the Carter place. Hod and Dora are dead. So are their guards," Philip bit out.

"When?"

"Can't say for sure. Maybe late yesterday. They were found early this morning by Pablo Gómez, who delivers fresh eggs every morning. He about rode the wheels off his wagon to get here," Rogers said.

"You know what they took?"

"No. I sent Kirby and three men out there. But as you know, Hod Carter was a retired gold-miner and I know he had a safe with I'd guess a lot of gold in it," Rogers said. His lips tightened as he spat the words out. "Bastards. Stinking, murdering bastards!"

"I'll go have a look right away."

"Good," Rogers said, and strode angrily into the house.

Fargo felt the accusation in Isabel's black-fire eyes as she peered at him. "Whatever it is, say it," he barked.

"You might have spotted them if you'd been riding the hills," she said, her lovely face fashioned of ice. "But you were too busy enjoying yourself."

"I can't cover the whole damn territory, and I don't aim to. I might not have come on a damn thing," he returned.

"But you might have," she insisted, and he cursed silently, unable to refute the element of truth in her accusation, slim as it was.

He turned the Ovaro and rode off. "I'll be back," he flung over his shoulder as the pinto went into a gallop. He rode hard and finally reached the Carter place. He slowed and scanned the three rock sides again as he moved down the one path to the house. One of the guards lay slain near the top of the path.

Fargo rode by and halted in front of the house, where Alden Kirby and two of his men stood a few paces away from two blanket-covered forms on the ground.

"The undertaker's on his way," Kirby said.

"This is where they were found, I take it," Fargo said, and Kirby nodded.

"You know what was taken?" Fargo questioned.

"They blew the safe open in the study. I guess they took all the gold Hod Carter had there," Kirby answered.

Fargo kept the distaste from his face as he uncovered the bodies of Hod and Dora Carter, and his eyes were narrowed as he peered at the still forms. He examined the bullet wounds, let his eyes sweep the ground on all sides of their bodies, and felt the grimness inside himself as he pulled the blankets back in place. He turned to the three bodies of the slain guards that dotted the ground near the rear corner of the house. They had been killed as they ran from the back of the house when they heard the first shots, each of them facing the bodies of Hod and Dora Carter.

His lips a thin line, Fargo turned from the three bodies to see Alden Kirby in the saddle.

"I'm on my way to High River. Mr. Rogers told me to meet him there at Saint Mary's," Kirby said. "My men will wait for the undertaker."

Fargo nodded, watched Kirby ride off at a fast canter, and then slowly climbed the pathway to the house to where the first sentry lay dead. He bent down as his eyes scanned the still form. The man lay facing the house, but the bullet had gone into his back, the red stain unmistakable just over his belt.

Fargo rose and let his gaze scan the pathway as he walked back to the Ovaro. Whatever prints there had been had been obliterated by the hoofprints of Kirby and his men. He pulled himself onto the pinto, took another long glance at the scene, and slowly rode from the place. He climbed a low hill well covered by white fir. He found a level pathway and rode, and he knew the furrow stayed on his brow as he thought about what he'd found at the Carter place.

He broke off thoughts as he realized that the heavy tree cover at his right had suddenly become a very silent place. The chatter of white-breasted nuthatches had been loud, along with the noisy sounds of gold-finches, and now suddenly everything was quiet.

Instinctively, he edged closer to the nearest trees when a shot exploded the stillness. The bullet slammed into a low branch only a fraction of an inch from his head, and he felt the shower of splinters as he dived from the saddle. He hit the ground, rolled hard into a tree trunk, and skittered around to the other side. He lay flattened, the Colt in his hand, and waited for another shot, but there was none. Finally, he rose to one knee and carefully peered up into the thick tree cover of the hill. His eyes swept the trees that rose up above him, searched for the quiver of leaves, the movement of a branch.

But there was nothing. His assailant had fired one shot, probably from afoot, and left, unwilling to risk another. But the first one had been close, too damned close, Fargo thought as he rose to his feet. He walked to the tree branch gouged out by the bullet, saw the heaviest impact where the bullet had plowed into it, and drew an imaginary trajectory line into the trees. The shot had come from slightly ahead of where he'd been riding, he decided.

He climbed back onto the Ovaro and began to move carefully up through the trees. He followed the line he'd drawn in his mind, the big Colt in one hand ready to fire. But he found no one. He hadn't really expected he would, and he reached the top of the hill to find that the land leveled off in a high plain well-covered with mountain brush and hawthorn, ground too tangled to pick up a trail.

He made his way back down the hill and continued on toward the Rogers' ranch. In the distance, a line of brown-robed figures shuffled along a narrow path, each with a basket in one hand. He paused to watch them gather greens, probably lamb's-quarters, purslane, and strawberry spinach, though he'd also noticed mustard growing tall in the area.

He rode on and reached the Rogers' place to see Isabel in one of the corrals, using the lunge line on the same stallion. The horse was giving her trouble, a wild-eyed dark-gray Arabian with an angry flare to its nostrils. Two ranch hands were standing by, he noted, and Isabel halted as she saw him ride up. She tossed the lunge line to one of the hands and crawled through the fence beams to hurry over to him.

"Your father's gone to High River, I hear?" Fargo said.

"Yes, to see Father Malachy and make funeral arrangements for Hod and Dora. They were regulars and heavy patrons of St. Mary's," she said. "You find out anything?"

"A few things," he said. "They didn't try to fight or run. There was no sign of any struggle."

"Meaning what?"

"Someone they knew or trusted came down that one way into their place. They greeted whoever it was and were killed on the spot," Fargo said, and saw the shock slide across her face.

"And the guards?"

"The ones by the house were killed when they came running. The one at the top of the path was shot when he turned around, by whoever went down to meet the Carters."

Isabel turned the words in her mind, her black eyes steady on him. "You're pointing at one of the ranch managers again, someone from inside," she said.

He shrugged. "Someone they trusted. That's all I'm saying. Could've been the man that delivers the eggs," he said.

"You know it wasn't him. He called us," Isabel said.

"I know that," Fargo said. "But someone they knew, someone they trusted."

"That could include other deliverymen, gardeners, even friends as well as ranch managers." Isabel frowned.

"That's right," Fargo agreed. "This gang has a point man, somebody, somewhere. I'd guess the same person who took a shot at me after I left the Carter place. Almost made it a bull's-eye."

Surprise leapt into Isabel's face, then a touch of smugness. "Well, that lets out Alden. He was at the Carters'," she said.

"He'd left to go to High River to meet your father. He had plenty of time to pick a spot and wait for me," Fargo said.

"Dammit, why do you keep accusing Alden?" Isabel flared.

"I'm not accusing him. I'm saying it was possible," Fargo said calmly.

"Anything's possible," she flung back, and strode into the house. He watched her go and knew he had been correct about her and Alden Kirby. No affair. No man-woman involvement. She just couldn't accept the monstrousness of the possibility. Or she was listening to her very acute, female intuition.

His eyes narrowed. He wouldn't discount the essence of that inner power. He'd seen it work too often. Yet he couldn't accept it either, not yet. He was only certain of one thing: these bandits were not the ordinary thieving band of renegades. From the stark terror they'd thrown into Magdalena's uncle to their cleverness and precision, they were something different.

He led the pinto to the side of the house, draped the reins over a fence post, and paused as he glanced at the spot where Magdalena usually parked the road cart. It wasn't there, and he walked to the rear door and entered, glanced into the kitchen, strolled to the room where the big wooden vats of cleaning clothes were in a row. She wasn't in either place. He called her name, but no one answered. He walked from the house and saw the elderly manservant in his white jacket. "Do you know where Magdalena is?" he asked.

The man hesitated. "Ask Miss Isabel," he murmured, and hurried away.

Fargo felt the furrow touch his brow, and he strode to the front of the house to see Isabel walking toward the corral. "I was looking for Magdalena," he said.

"She's gone," Isabel said.

"Gone?"

"I dismissed her," she said, challenge in her stare.

"Dismissed her? What the hell for?"

"She was obviously a distraction," Isabel said loftily. "Now you can devote all your attention to what you were hired to do, day and night."

"Goddamn," Fargo rasped.

"You can spend your time riding the hills or here," Isabel said.

"You've your high-toned nerve," Fargo snapped. "I'm wondering what your real reasons were."

Her eyes shot black fire. "And I'm wondering if she didn't make sure you were with her last night when the Carters were hit," Isabel flung back. "Maybe her uncle wasn't running from something he saw. Maybe he was one of them and they had had a falling out and he had to run. It happens often with thieves, I'm told."

"You're reaching, honey."

"Don't you think it strange he never told Magdalena what had shocked him so badly?"

"A man scared out of his wits doesn't talk," Fargo said. "Besides, all this is nothing but a damn excuse."

"For what?"

"For firing her. You might even believe that little tale you've just run through, but that's not why you sent her packing. You're just plain jealous of her," he threw at Isabel.

"Me jealous of her? Preposterous."

"You're jealous of the way she's honest and real about herself, and the sad thing is that you don't even know it."

"You're out of line, Fargo," she said, retreating into her shell of authority.

"You hire Magdalena back or I'm on my way, honey."

"I don't take ultimatums."

"Look at it as a warm gesture. Look at it as correcting a mistake. Look at it any damn way you want, but do it," he said, his last words harsh as any rock-scrabble cliff. He waited while she turned away, her finely etched lips pressed hard against each other.

"All right," she murmured finally. "Father needs you. Tell her she's expected back in the morning."

He nodded. He'd won, and he knew how hard it had been for her to agree. It was probably the first time she'd given in on anything. Concessions were new to her, defeat foreign, and all the more bitter because of it. He'd let her salvage something out of it. She was spoiled more than mean. "I'll be back. I'll stay the night here," he said, and caught the flash of gratefulness in her face before she wiped it away. "I'll bed down someplace on my own," he said.

"One of the small guest rooms looks out over the entire back of the ranch," she said. "I'll show you."

He followed and enjoyed the willow-wand walk of her swaying hips and firm, tight rear, controlled sensuousness in every line of her. The room, at a corner of the house, held a bed and small dresser, but its two windows almost touched each other and allowed a sweeping view of the stables, barns, corrals, and part of the front of the house.

"Good enough." He nodded and walked outside. He heard her following, quick steps to stay with his long-legged stride, and when he reached the Ovaro, she turned toward the corral. "Going to work with that Arabian again?" he asked, and she nodded. "Careful. He's made of meanness," he said, and she nodded thanks at the advice.

He swung onto the pinto and rode from the ranch, settled down to a steady trot along the hillside that led to Magdalena's place. He found himself thinking about Isabel's words—angry, spearing accusations about Magdalena's uncle. He didn't believe them, yet he couldn't dismiss anything that held even the shadow of possibility, whether it was Alden Kirby or Pedro. He'd file it away, one of the dark thoughts that had to remain.

When he reached Magdalena's, she hugged herself against him at once. "You heard?" she asked, and he nodded.

"I've something to tell you," he said, and she listened as he told her most of his exchange with Isabel. When he finished, she nodded soberly.

"Perhaps she is right. It is best you stay at the ranch these nights," Magdalena said. "But I will be here waiting whenever you can come."

"I know," he said, and when he left, the taste of her full lips was on his, the pressure of her big, pillowy breasts still warm against his chest.

It was dusk when he reached the Rogers' ranch and saw Isabel leaving the corral as two cowhands herded the Arabian into the stable with two rope halters on him. He frowned as she reached him, and he took in the dirt-smudged bruise along her temple, her ebony hair disarranged and her face shiny with perspiration. A tear ran along one shoulder of her shirt.

"It spun on me, knocked me into the corral fence. I fell and its hoove missed me. It turned when the men rushed at it," she said.

Fargo's eyes stayed on her. "You were lucky," he commented. "I'm glad to see you're all right. Glad to see something else, too." She frowned a question at him. "You can look like ordinary folks, all mussed up, things out of place, sweaty and grimy," he said. "I didn't think it was possible."

"You're not likely to see it again," she sniffed, and strode into the house. He turned to see Philip Rogers and Kirby ride in with the night.

"Services tomorrow," Rogers said, pain and exhaustion in his face. "You come up with anything?"

"I told Isabel. She can fill you in," Fargo said, and Philip nodded and hurried into the house. Kirby walked away, headed for his quarters.

Fargo strolled to the little guest room at the corner of the house. He stretched across the bed and left the lamp out to lay in the darkness until the ranch grew quiet, the sounds from the bunkhouse drifting into silence. He rose and quietly led the Ovaro across the yard in front of the house as the moon rose high. He was about to swing onto the saddle when he glimpsed the dark figure just outside the front of the house. He dropped into a crouch, the Colt half out of its holster

73

when the figure moved and became a slender, willow-wand shape. He dropped the gun back into its holster and stepped forward. Isabel wore a filmy shawl over the silk nightgown and her black eyes met his as he halted in front of her.

"Couldn't sleep," she said. "You promised you'd be staying here."

"Or in the hills," he corrected. "I keep my word."

Her lips tightened at the reproof in his tone, and she half-shrugged. "Apologies," she murmured.

"You always so suspicious?"

She blinked and he caught the honest confusion in her voice. "No, not at all. I don't know why I'm being this way now."

"Maybe you're just upset in general."

"Kindness?" she returned, and he shrugged. "I'll take it," she said. "Thank you. It might be being upset, but that's not all of it."

"What's the rest?"

"I don't know. I'll tell you when I do."

"Fair enough," he said. He swung onto the Ovaro and felt her eyes hard on him.

"Be careful."

"Always," he answered, and rode from her at a slow trot. She wasn't all that sure of herself, he decided. The regal posture was at least partly a defense. But he put Isabel Rogers from his mind and concentrated on his path into the hills. Things always appeared different at night, but he found the places he had marked in his mind, kept climbing, and finally he was standing on the small, flat ledge of rock. He had spotted it as he rode during the day. Even in the pale moonlight, it allowed a commanding view of most of the land below. Perhaps even more important, sounds from below traveled upward with astounding clarity, the hills acting as a kind of funnel.

He dismounted and stretched out with his back against an alder. His eyes scanned the land below in long, slow sweeps, and he dozed from time to time, certain that the sound of even one rider would spiral up to him. But the night stayed quiet, save for the usual night sounds, the soft swish of brush as deer passed by, the chatter of kit foxes, and the call of the nighthawk.

He was awake when the dawn came, the sun edging the tops of the high Sierra peaks to finally roll downward like a warm yellow blanket unfolding. He rose and slowly made his way downhill and back to the Rogers' ranch.

Isabel, still in a bathrobe, appeared outside the house as he dismounted, took the saddle from the Ovaro, and started for the corner guest room. "Fargo," she called, and he crossed to where she waited. "You said you'd come to Saint Mary's some morning. Come to the service with us this afternoon. You'll have till noon to rest."

"Why not?" he agreed, and went on to the room. He undressed and quickly fell asleep across the bed until, just before the noon hour, he woke. He washed, changed shirts, and when he went outside, Philip Rogers and Isabel sat in the front seat of a fixed top Brunswick, graceful of line, painted a deep maroon. Isabel wore a black gown that sheathed her willowy shape, her father in a black frock coat. Alden Kirby was in the saddle on the other side of the carriage, and Fargo brought the pinto alongside Rogers.

"Isabel filled me in. Sharp deductions, Fargo. But who did the Carters trust? There are so many possibilities," Rogers said as he put the carriage in motion.

"Somebody from one of the villages," Kirby snapped. "Somebody they employed once. I tell you the gang's made up of the damn Mexican peasants."

Rogers glanced at Fargo. "I can't rule it out," the Trailsman said.

"You don't rule it out, but you don't do anything about it," Kirby snapped.

"That's right," Fargo said quietly. "Everybody knows what you think, Kirby. You've said it loud enough and often enough. The Carters knew it. They'd have been careful about ex-workmen coming in."

"Maybe not, Fargo," Philip Rogers put in. "The man who delivered the eggs found them. They'd have trusted him. There may have been someone else."

"One of us, that's what Fargo thinks," Kirby interjected. "One of the ranch managers they'd trust all the way."

"I can't rule it out, either," Fargo said with quiet doggedness.

"Go to hell, mister," Kirby shot back. "I'll get to the bottom of this, not you."

"That's enough, Alden," Rogers admonished, and the rest of the trip was made in silence. When they reached High River, Fargo glanced at the sun. It had taken a good hour with the carriage. A horse and rider could do it in half that. He made a mental note with no special reason in mind. It was a habit. Mental notes came in handy at unexpected times.

The church was instantly visible, the tower rising high over the low-roofed buildings of the rest of the town. Surreys, traps, and standing-top phaetons were among the carriages that lined the front of the church.

Fargo tethered the Ovaro and followed the others inside. He halted to take in the quiet, dignified opulence of the interior of the church. Walls decorated with mosaics, statues of various saints in recessed niches, carved columns of stone, and dark wood, polished pews. Tall, silver candleholders held slowly burning, thick white candles, and as Fargo lowered himself into one of the pews beside Isabel, he took in the pure-white cloth with gold trim that covered the altar and the dark-red carpet over the altar steps. A gleaming gold chalice occupied the center of the altar, but the most impressive piece was the large cross against the wall over the altar. Made of wood, the cross was studded with glistening pieces of stone, each in its own silver setting.

Fargo peered at the stones as he whispered to Isabel, "Are those what I think they are?" he asked.

"Yes," she whispered back. "Rubies, emeralds, diamonds, sapphires."

"Jade, topaz, and pieces of gold," he finished.

"The cross was made by Spanish craftsmen hundreds of years ago," Isabel said, and fell silent as the priest appeared in his black robes and began the service in flowing Latin.

Unable to understand any of it, Fargo found himself thinking of the chapel at the mission with the stone, unadorned altar, the backless benches, and the simple wooden cross on the wall. The contrast was stark, almost beyond reconciling, but he had often heard that the Church was different things to different people. Opulence for some, stark simplicity for others. He certainly wasn't fit to judge ancient wisdoms, he mused, and he remembered someone once saying that it wasn't the cover of a book but the message inside that mattered.

As the service went on, the priest and his acolytes performing their rites before the altar, Fargo let himself count the precious stones in the huge cross. Twenty in all, he murmured when he finished, a fortune in gems. But the service came to a close and he rose with Isabel and everyone else and filed from the church. Isabel waited outside until the priest came out, talked to the others, and finally found his way to her. Fargo took in a man of medium height, grayish hair with bright-blue eyes and a firm jaw set in a strong face.

When Isabel and the priest finished their conversation, she steered the man over to where Fargo waited. "Fargo, this is Father Malachy," she introduced. "Fargo's the man Father hired to stop the killing and stealing."

"Any progress?" Father Malachy asked.

"Some. Not enough, though."

The priest appraised him with a long glance. "You're not a man to give up, I'm thinking," he said. "You'll catch them."

"Any vote of confidence is welcome." Fargo smiled. With a few more words to Philip Rogers, Father Malachy returned to the church and Isabel climbed into the Brunswick. Fargo drew the Ovaro alongside as Philip turned to his daughter.

"The Dodds asked me to go back to their place with them. Do you mind if Fargo sees you home, my dear?" he asked.

"Not at all," Isabel said as she slid over and took the reins.

Fargo watched Alden Kirby go with Rogers, and he fell in beside the carriage as Isabel drove away. When they reached the road back through the low hills, she tossed him an almost sly smile.

"Any thoughts?" she asked.

"It's a rich man's church, all right," he remarked.

"Because you see only the surface things. As run by the Jesuits, it's a place of learning as well as worship, a place of the mind as well as the spirit," Isabel said. "It's a church for those who appreciate the traditional, the beauty of ritual, the elegance of Latin. It's not for everyone."

"You're something," Fargo said.

"Meaning what exactly?"

"You're even a snob about religion."

"Go to hell, Fargo," she flared, and snapped the reins. He put the pinto into a trot and stayed alongside her until she slowed down. "It's not being a snob," she flung at him. "You don't understand."

"Guess not, honey."

"It's being brought up to accept only the very best, to appreciate the rare. It's being raised not to compromise or lower your standards."

"That's part of it. It's also being raised to think you're better than anyone else, and that's no damn good," Fargo said, and she fell silent again until they reached the ranch. He waited as Isabel stepped down and turned the carriage over to one of the ranch hands.

She came over to where he had dismounted, and her black eyes searched his face. "I stand by the things I said. I don't think that makes me a snob. I don't mean to be a snob. Does that make any sense?"

"Maybe."

"Do you understand what I'm trying to say?" she asked, no disdain in her voice.

"I'm working on it," he allowed. She nodded thoughtfully, turned, and walked into the house. Beneath the surface, she wrestled with her own uncertainties, he realized. Raised to believe in the superiority of the aristocracy, she also knew the twists and turns of the line between right and wrong, truth and the mere appearance of truth. He gave her credit for recognizing that, if not yet admitting anything.

He unsaddled the Ovaro as night swept down from the high Sierras and used the body brush from his saddlebag to clear the road scuff from the horse's coat and mane. He had just finished when the elderly manservant in the white jacket appeared. He carried a tray of food and a glass of wine. "Compliments of Miss Isabel," he said.

"Much obliged, tell her." Fargo nodded and carried the tray to a flat tree stump, where he leisurely ate and watched the ranch hands drift into the bunkhouse after stabling all the horses. The man returned to collect the tray, and Fargo walked to the corral fence and let his eyes sweep the front of the main house. He could see Isabel's room at the other end of the house and glimpsed her inside. Finally, he strolled to the guest room at the other corner of the hcuse, undressed, and stretched out on the bed. He heard Philip Rogers and Kirby return, and finally the ranch fell silent. He had seen the night sentries in the positions he had assigned them close to the house, and he let sleep come to him in the soft luxury of the bed.

The night had grown deep when he snapped awake at the explosion of gunfire. Leaping from the bed, he ran to the window and saw the horses running out of the stables and into the corrals. More shots and shouts erupted and he glimpsed at least four men on horseback racing up and down at the corrals. The guards were moving forward, firing wildly as more Arabians raced from the stable and then other figures streamed from the bunkhouse. Suddenly, he saw the yellow glow that meant only one thing: hay set afire. He heard Philip Rogers' voice screaming, "The horses. They're stealing the horses. Spread out to the ends of the corrals. Stop them. Water buckets, goddammit, water buckets."

Fargo spun from the window. "Shit," he spit out as he yanked on boots, trousers, and gun belt. He ran from the room, but instead of going outside, he streaked down the long corridors of the house to Isabel's room. He crashed the door open without slowing

*80*

a step, and saw the three figures at the window. One had Isabel slung over his shoulder, another already outside the window to help lift her out, and the third standing by. All three men turned as the Trailsman crashed into the room. Fargo couldn't shoot without fear of hitting Isabel and he saw the third man bring up his six-gun.

Fargo felt the bullet go over his head as he dived forward, hit the floor rolling, and kept rolling. The man got off another shot, fired too fast, and Fargo heard the bullet slam into the floor. He continued to roll and slammed into the man's ankles. "Goddamn," the man swore as, knocked off-balance, he pitched forward. Fargo's shot, from underneath, tore into the falling man's belly, and the figure collapsed half atop him with a groaning sound. As Fargo pushed out from under the dead man, the other one holding Isabel turned toward him. She had been knocked out, Fargo saw, her figure hanging limply in the white silk nightgown. He started to bring his gun up but saw the boot that kicked out at his face. He managed to twist away, but the blow still caught him against the temple and he went sprawling. Pain and flashing colors exploded in his head as he hit the floor and rolled—a subconscious reflex. The flashing colors went away and he saw the man starting to pass Isabel through the window to the third one outside.

Leaping from the floor in an upward, diving tackle, he slammed into the man behind his knees, and the figure buckled and went down. Fargo saw the third man outside yank Isabel's limp form through the window, get one shoulder under her, and hoist her up. Fargo raised the Colt and aimed, but lowered the gun as the man ran toward a horse, Isabel's inert body hanging across his back. Fargo heard the sound behind him, whirled, and saw the man lift a six-gun to fire.

He dropped and the bullet plowed into the windowsill a fraction of an inch from his head. His answering shot caught the man full in the chest and he flew backward as though kicked by a mule.

Fargo spun and vaulted through the window to see the third man depositing Isabel over the saddle of a horse. But a shot could go through him and hit the young woman as she lay head-down across the saddle. He had to get the man to step away from her. He dropped to one knee, the Colt aimed and ready to fire. "Don't move," he shouted, and as he expected, the man did just the opposite. He whirled, gun in hand, and took a precious few seconds to locate his target. They were his last few seconds. As he whirled, he moved a few inches away from Isabel and Fargo's shot caught him at the base of the throat. A fountain of red flew from his mouth as he pitched forward to hit the ground on his face.

Fargo rose and glanced toward the corral. The shooting had stopped and there were ranch hands trying to calm the excited horses while other threw buckets of water on the bale of burning hay. The attackers had broken away as soon as they'd fired the initial shots and set the hay on fire. He walked toward the horse just as Isabel regained consciousness, and he pulled her from the saddle. Her eyes held his for a moment and then she was leaning hard against his naked chest, a small tremor coursing through her. He felt the soft warmth of her breasts against him and the willow slenderness of her body under his hands. Yet there was a strength to it, he realized, no will-o'-the-wisp frailness.

She pulled back to look up at him. "You knew," she murmured. "That's why you reached me in time."

He nodded and she hugged herself tight against him again. "You'd best use one of the guest rooms for the rest of the night. Your room will need some cleaning up."

"Let me get something to put on," she said, and he went with her into the house, her arm tightly locked in his, the small points atop each breast pressing into the silk fabric as she walked. She avoided the blood-soaked figures on the floor of her bedroom as she gathered clothes and stepped behind a screen. She emerged in a light-green shirt and black skirt, the nightgown on her arm. She went outside with him, her arm in his again, and Fargo saw that the hay fire had been mostly doused and the ranch hands were busy calming the horses.

Philip Rogers strode toward him, Kirby following behind. "Dammit, Fargo, where the hell have you been?" the man glowered. "They attacked, tried to steal the horses."

"He's been saving my life, that's where he's been, Father," Isabel said, and Rogers turned to her with a frown. The frown became shock as Isabel told him how the three man had seized her.

Rogers turned his eyes to Fargo when she finished, a plainly shaken man. "Good God. My apologies, Fargo," he said.

"They weren't after the horses. That was a smoke screen, a diversion so that they could snatch Isabel," Fargo said.

"How did you know?" the man asked.

"They don't steal horses. They can only handle small things—money, gold, coins—things they can carry and hide away somewhere," Fargo said. "They were going to hold Isabel for ransom."

"And I'd have paid it, of course," Rogers said. "They knew that."

"Maybe with the same result as if you didn't pay,"

Fargo said, and watched his words sink into Philip Rogers.

"My God," the man half-croaked. "Thank God you realized what they were doing, Fargo."

"Search the three I killed, though I don't expect you'll find anything that'll help," Fargo said.

"I still say they're from the peasant villages," Alden Kirby muttered.

Rogers put an arm around his daughter's shoulder. "I'll fix you a hot brandy, my dear."

"I'll be right in," Isabel said, and her father went into the house. Kirby drifted away. She came forward, flattened her palms against Fargo's naked chest. "I wish I were better at saying thank you," she murmured.

"Work on it," he said blandly.

She reached up and her lips brushed his cheek, a quick, feathery touch. "I will," she said, and hurried into the house.

Fargo returned to the little corner room, shed the few clothes he had on, and lay down on the bed, his brow furrowed and he finally fell asleep.

# 5

Fargo was still puzzled when he woke in the morning, but sleep had brought some of his thoughts into focus. The attempt at kidnapping Isabel had almost worked. Another attempt might succeed. More important, he hadn't any clue as to where they might strike next. Nor did he have a way of getting a lead, yet. That was the core of the problem. They held all the cards, he realized as he washed and dressed. Somehow, someway, that had to be changed.

Rogers was outside with Kirby when Fargo walked toward the stables. "You were right. They hadn't a scrap of identification on them," Rogers said. "But they weren't Mexican."

"Hired help. Special job. Special help," Kirby said.

Fargo shrugged, unable to dismiss the possibility, but he gave it little weight. These bandits were a tight-knit group, not the kind to hire outside help. "How's Isabel?" he asked Rogers.

"Sleeping late," the man answered.

"Understandable," Fargo said, and went on to saddle the Ovaro. He saw Magdalena as he brought the horse out. She waved at him. Before riding out he paused at the corrals and scanned the ground. There were too many hoofprints to pick up a trail.

He sent the pinto on in a slow trot and rode into the low hills with his lips a thin line as he turned toward the mission. He was riding casually, letting thoughts idle inside his mind, when he saw the two rows of brown-robed figures, some atop a ridge, the other below in a narrow cleft of land. All had their little baskets with them, and he spied the cross on the chest of the first figure atop the ridge and sent the pinto up the steep incline. Father Junípero halted and turned to him as he reached the ridge. "I was on my way to see you," Fargo said.

"Then you have been spared the trip," Father Junípero said.

"Have the brothers heard anything to help me?" Fargo asked.

"I am afraid not, only that everyone is afraid," the padre said.

"The people of the villages afraid? But these *bandidos* are only hitting at those with something to steal," Fargo said.

"But many of the people work at the big ranches or sell things to them. They have heard the talk that some feel that the *bandidos* are from the village people. They are afraid the rich ranchers will fire them and stop trading with them."

"What do you think about that maybe being true, that the gang is from the villages?" Fargo questioned.

Father Junípero's lined face took on almost a sadness. "It is not for me to point a finger in judgment, my son," he said. "I can only hope such thoughts are wrong." He blessed himself and moved on, the other friars obediently following.

Fargo turned words in his mind. It had been a disturbing reply. He would not point the finger of judgment, Father Junípero had said, yet in the reply he had done just that. Perhaps the good friars had heard things their compassion refused to allow them to say.

Dissatisfied, Fargo rode the hills again in the off chance that he might pick up a trail. The attackers had scattered as soon as their diversion was finished, he was certain, and by the day's end he had found nothing to offer a lead of any sort.

It was dusk when he returned to the Rogers' ranch and saw Isabel hurry from the house to greet him. "We have to talk," she said, her voice tight. "I'm concerned."

"Over what?"

"Alden," she said. "He's been talking all day about whatever Magdalena's uncle saw being the key to it. He's convinced she knows more than she's told anyone."

"You were thinking along those lines," Fargo reminded her.

"Yes, but I think Alden's gone to Magdalena's place to try to force whatever she knows from her. He's determined to show you up," Isabel said. "I'm afraid for Magdalena. Maybe she knows something. Maybe she doesn't. But this isn't the way to find out."

"Good girl," Fargo said as he wheeled the Ovaro and put the horse into a gallop. He kept the powerful, ground-eating stride until he came in sight of Magdalena's place. Night had descended and he slowed the pinto to a walk as he saw Kirby's horse near the open doorway of the house.

Fargo slid from the saddle and landed on the balls of his feet as he heard Magdalena's cry of pain. He was at the doorway in three long strides and saw Kirby had her on the floor, one hand wrapped around her thick, curly black hair as he yanked her head back.

"He told me nothing," Magdalena cried out. "Nothing."

"I don't believe you. Either you tell me what you know or I'll beat it out of you," Kirby said. "You'll never work for Rogers again if you don't cooperate with me."

"I don't know anything," she repeated, and yelped as Kirby yanked on her hair.

"Let go of her, you goddamn fool," Fargo said with deadly quiet, and he saw the surprise flood Alden Kirby's face as the man looked up.

"You get out of here. I'm handling this, Fargo. She's got you fooled," Kirby said, but he took his hand from Magdalena's hair and straightened up.

"You've three seconds to get on your horse, or I'm going to give you a new face, one you won't like," Fargo said.

Kirby's mouth grew tight. "Goddamn, I've had enough of you, Fargo," he said, came forward, and threw a looping right.

Fargo got an arm up, deflected the punch, started his own blow to the head, and Kirby raised his arm to parry it. Fargo's punch changed directions and slammed into the man's abdomen, and Kirby let out a gasp of pain as he doubled over. A left hook caught him on the point of the chin and he sailed backward, to land a foot from the open doorway.

His eyes glazed, he struggled to his feet. Fargo's blow slammed into the side of his face. A thin spray of red erupted where the skin of Kirby's cheekbone split as he flew backward through the doorway. The Trailsman was outside after him instantly, but Kirby lay still, his head to one side. Fargo pulled him up by one arm, lifted him, and threw him across the saddle of his horse. He sent the mount into a canter with a sharp slap on its rump and strode into the house.

Magdalena clutched her arms around him at once. "Will he come back?" she asked.

"No, that's not Kirby's style," Fargo said. "And I'll see he never bothers you again."

"I am so lucky you came by."

"I was told he'd maybe be here," Fargo said. "Isabel told me." Magdalena's eyes widened in surprise. "There is more to her than seems. Maybe more than she knows herself," he said.

"I am glad," Magdalena said gravely. "And grateful to her for sending you. I will tell her tomorrow."

"Do that," Fargo said, and held Magdalena tight as her mouth found his.

"I will still be here waiting," she said as she walked outside with him.

"I haven't forgotten," he said, and slowly rode into the dark of the night. He moved through a line of spruce, stayed in the trees, probably an unnecessary precaution, yet he decided to be cautious. He rode with thoughts sorting themselves in his mind, and he had made one decision before he reached the ranch. The gang had all the advantanges this way. Place, time, surprise, target, all in their hands. He was reduced to waiting, hoping to pick up a trail afterward, and that was no good. Waiting never caught anyone. He had to do more, make something happen. He had to make them come out, on his terms. He had to pick the time and place.

The decision firm in his mind, he reached the ranch and dismounted, unsaddled the Ovaro, and returned from the stable just as Isabel came outside. "You were in time," she said.

"How do you know?" he asked.

"I saw Alden come in," she said, her small smile making any further words unnecessary. "What, now?" she asked.

"See me in the morning," he said. "I've got to do some more thinking." She nodded and turned to go when he caught her arm. "That was a nice thing you did tonight," he said.

She offered a wry smile. "I'm learning," she said. "Good night, Fargo."

He let her go on and strolled to the corner guest room at the other end of the house. He undressed and lay across the bed as he let his mind review everything he had concluded about the gang so far. Slowly, plans took shape and gathered details to themselves. When he finally closed his eyes in sleep, he had gone as far as he could with thoughts. The rest would depend on whether he could turn plans into reality. That, he knew, was the hard part.

He slept soundly, and the sun was a warm, golden stream of light that flooded the room when he woke. When he finished dressing, he went outside and saw Isabel approaching with a mug of coffee in each hand. She offered him one and he drank the hot, bracing brew.

"I told Father about last night. He's already told Alden it's still your show and to back off. Of course, there's no guarantee Alden will do that. He's an angry man."

"My little talk with him last night may hold more weight."

"Finish your thinking?" Isabel asked over the rim of her coffee mug.

"For now," Fargo said. "I'm going to pay a visit to Saint Mary's."

Her eyes grew wide. "You're going to Saint Mary's? Why?"

"You want to catch a fox you've got to think like a fox," Fargo said, and saw Isabel's questioning frown stay. "The precious stones in that big cross are made for this gang of cutthroats. I'm sure that's on their list of targets."

"You're going to warn Father Malachy?" Isabel said.

"No. I'm going to have him help set a trap," Fargo said. "I want to move the cross out of the church to a safer place. I want him to announce that he's going to do that. They can't sit back and let that happen."

"Father Malachy won't move the cross," Isabel said. "It will be against his principles."

"Come along with me. Maybe you can help," Fargo said.

"I'll come along, but I don't think I'll be much help. I'll get my horse," she said, took his cup, and returned it to the house. He watched her come back, changed into a white shirt and tan riding britches. She hurried into the stable, emerged on the light-gray, beautiful Arabian, and rode beside him as he set out on a slow trot. "I don't understand one thing. You said they only took small things they could carry off and hide away. It takes three men to carry that cross," she said.

"They can pry those precious stones out of it in a matter of minutes," Fargo said.

"Thinking like a fox," Isabel said with a wry smile. He nodded, and she cast a sidelong glance at him. "Seeing through another person's eyes, thinking through another person's mind. You do that a lot, I'd guess," she mused aloud. "It's strange, but somehow you've made me do that, in small way, of course. I find myself looking at people differently, trying to understand them, to see the world as they see it. I've never done that."

"It helps you understand yourself better, too."

"Yes, so it does," she said, and he felt the unsaid hanging in her words.

"Such as?"

"You said Magdalena isn't afraid to be honest with

91

herself, another way of saying I am," Isabel reminded him.

"Some women use their beauty as a defense, a shield," he said. "It keeps everything at arm's length, including their own feelings."

"You think that's what I do?"

"You tell me," he countered, and she offered no reply.

She turned her horse and rode up a narrow pathway into the high hills, a sudden move that had him following in surprise. When she halted he found himself in an arbor of white fir, cool and shaded, yet with a view of the terrain for miles below.

"Father Malachy won't be at the church till noon. He's at the school in the mornings," she said as she dismounted. "There's no sense in getting there early and waiting around."

"Guess not," Fargo agreed, and swung from the pinto.

"I used to come up here when I was younger and wanted to be alone," she said. "It was a time of growing up, thinking about yourself, about your body, about boys. It seems a long time ago, and now suddenly I find I'm thinking about myself again, about being real and honest. All your fault, Fargo."

"You tossing out blame or credit?" he asked, and she laughed, the sound low and husky.

"Both," she said, turned toward him, and suddenly her arms were around his neck, her finely etched lips pressing hard against his mouth. "Oh, God," he heard her breathe as she kissed him again, harder, seeming to pull her arms back yet clinging to him. Her hands moved under the top of his shirt, pulled buttons open, and caressed his chest, pausing to press against his nipples. "Oh, God," she murmured again, and he felt his shirt slide from his shoulders as her hands roamed over his muscled torso with almost frantic abandon.

He cupped a hand under one breast and she gasped. He tore the buttons on her shirt open, to close his fingers around the soft, upwardly curved breast. "Oh, God," she murmured, each time with added breathlessness. He pulled her shirt off, snapped skirt buttons open, and slid garments down. She closed her legs and brought her knees up together as she half-turned away from him. Gently, he brought her legs back, still together, and took in the long-waisted, willow-wand beauty of her, breasts curving up in a sweeping line, each tipped by a nipple of light pink on a circle of matching pastel pink. Narrow hips with a flat abdomen and a tiny belly-button; her thighs, still held together, couldn't hide the curly, jet-black triangle of wiry firmness with little tendrils of hair resting against her thighs.

He brought his lips down to one pink nipple, pulled gently, sucked it into his mouth, and Isabel gave a high-pitched cry. "God, oh, God, oh, Jesus," she gasped out, and he felt her hands pressing against his body, moving up and down his skin, exploring, caressing. She came to his erect, throbbing maleness, touched its warmth, and screamed. He reached down, held her hand against him, closed her fingers around his pulsating wanting, and Isabel's cry became a wailing sound made of pure pleasure.

He brought his hand away, but she kept hold of him. She rubbed, pressed, pulled, and all the while pressed her breast deep into his mouth. "God, God, oh, yes, yes . . . aaaah, aaaah, oh, oh, oh," she screamed, and he felt her long, willowy thighs fall open as her body arched. He reached down, touched the wiry jet triangle, and she half-cried, half-laughed as he found the lubricious lips of absolute, consummate softness. He slid his finger gently, caressed and explored. Isabel's head tossed from side to side, her long jet hair flying in a wild rhythm as he moved over her and brought the tender-sweet throbbingness to the moist portal. She screamed, a long, lost wailing sound, even as her hands became little fists that pounded into his back.

The willow-wand legs closed around his hips and suddenly her high-pitched screams became low, throaty gasps as she arched against him, thrust upward, her hands pushed against his buttocks. "Yes, yes, more, more, give me, give me all of you," she said, suddenly finding words. "Oh, my God, my God, oh, please, yes, yes." The words became a torrent of sound, urging, pleading, praising, and all the while she pumped up with him in an ever-increasing frenzy. Her arms circled his neck and pulled his face onto the sweeping cups of pink-tipped softness.

Suddenly her thighs fell open, closed again, fell open, and slammed against his hips again. "Oh, my God, it's now . . . it's now . . . oh, God, it's happening, oh, dear Jesus, oh, oh, ooooooh," Isabel cried out, and he felt her contractions close around him. He was swept along with her, exploding with her as her head fell backward, the veins in her neck standing out against the whiteness of her skin.

She came with shaking, pounding ecstasy, and her voice wailed a hymn to the senses, pure pleasure in it yet an edge of wonder, a thread of discovery. When the world stopped its spinning, he heard her laugh as she clung to him. He lifted his lips from one soft cup and saw the smile on her finely etched lips as her black eyes bored into him as though she were trying to recognize someone she didn't know.

"It's me," he murmured, and she sobbed a laugh.

"I know," she whispered. "I was looking for myself."

She clung to him until he finally slid from her and she gave a shudder of final pleasure. He rose on one elbow and enjoyed the graceful, willow-wand loveliness of her as she lay with languorous satisfaction, one leg outstretched, the other half-bent. Finally, a smile curling her lips that was made of old truths and new wisdoms, she sat up and brushed her jet hair back with one hand, and he sat entranced by her beauty.

"Was that real enough? Honest enough?" she slid at him.

"It sure was."

She leaned back on both elbows and her upturned breasts seemed to reach for the warm sun. "One other time," she said almost abstractly.

"One time?"

"Yes. Everything under my control. All my doing. An experiment. Curiosity. No real pleasure. A little pain," she said as she thought back. "I was disappointed."

"You were bound to be."

"I always knew there had to be more," she said. "I was right." She slid herself against him, stretched her willowy body along his. "Someone I couldn't look down at, you said," she reminded him.

"Someone would have come along in time."

"Maybe. Maybe not. You came along now. That's all that matters."

"What matters is that we get to Saint Mary's," he said, and she drew away with a half-pout and began to pull on clothes.

He dressed, and when he rode down the hillside with her, he noticed a tightness had come into her face. "Concerned about meeting Father Malachy?" He smiled. "It won't show."

"Don't be smart," she snapped, but her quick smile told him he had struck home. He increased the pace and the town came into sight soon, the tall spire of the church easy to pick out. When they reined to a halt outside the church, Father Malachy came out in his cassock, his strong, square face breaking into a smile of surprise.

"Isabel," he exclaimed. "What brings you here today?"

"Fargo," she said simply with a nod at the big man beside her.

"Ah, yes, good to see you again, Fargo," the *padre* said. "Let's go inside."

Fargo cast a glance at the jewel-encrusted huge cross as he followed Father Malachy into a combination office and living room. "I want your help," the Trailsman began at once; he outlined his plan in quick, short sentences. "Moving the cross will be the bait. They'll take it, I'm sure."

"I'm sorry, I will not move the cross, not even for such a worthy plan," Father Malachy said. "I find the thought of doing so to be almost sacrilegious. It's as if the cross were fleeing from the forces of evil. That's an image I can't assimilate."

"I'm sure that in the long history of the Church, there have been times when the valuables of a cathedral were taken away before attacking hordes stole them," Fargo countered.

"Yes, when the Ottoman Turks besieged Vienna, when the Mongols reached the Danube Valley, to mention just two," Father Malachy said. "Ivory reliquaries, gold tabernacles and chalices, silver candlesticks, and jeweled exposition thrones, all these and more valuables were carried to safety. But never the cross, the symbol of Christianity. That has never fled."

Fargo shot a glance at Isabel, who shrugged helplessly. But he had suspected he might run into opposition and he allowed a smile of concession to Father Malachy. "How about playing along another way?" he said. "The cross stays. But you announce it's going to be moved to a safer place while those attacks are going on. Only we'll move a substitute cross, a piece of wood covered up. It'll look enough like the real thing to fool them."

He watched Father Malachy's eyes narrow in thought as he turned the proposition in his mind. Finally he brought his gaze back to Fargo. " 'The Lord cometh out of His place to punish the inhabitants of the earth for their iniquity.' Isaiah, twenty-six, twenty-one," Father Malachy said. "I suppose a little deception is in order to punish these sinners for their iniquities. I'll go along with you."

"Good," Fargo said. "At Sunday's Mass you'll announce you're moving the cross one night that week. I'll have the friars announce it, too, at the mission services."

"Why?" Isabel cut in.

"Kirby keeps saying the bandits are from the Mexican villages. Let's be sure everybody gets the news," Fargo said.

"There is a large, unfinished wooden cross in the crypt," Father Malachy said. "It should fit your purposes."

"Good. I'll stop by to wrap it up," Fargo said. "We'll spring the trap Wednesday night. Meanwhile, we three will be the only ones who know what's really going on. Agreed?"

"You have my word," the priest said, and Fargo rose, waited while Isabel said good-bye to the *padre* and moved outside to the horses.

"Just we three?" she said as she rode beside him, and he caught the edge in her voice.

"Don't go getting your nose out of joint. I trust

97

your father completely," Fargo said. "But even a trustworthy man can let a wrong word drop, a slip of the tongue, a mistake. The fewer people know about this, the fewer chances of that happening."

"I guess so," she conceded after a moment. "I just feel a little disloyal."

"Don't. He'll be playing an important part. Making sure we pull it off is all that counts," Fargo said, and saw her accept his words.

When they returned to the ranch as dusk settled in, she stood by as he told Philip Rogers everything but the key heart of the plan. "The cross will be moved Wednesday night. I'll need enough men to spring the trap. Can you have Dodd, Stove, Ben Dorrance, and Abel Cox each supply five good men?"

"Yes, of course," Rogers said.

"With the five you bring we'll have enough," Fargo said.

"You feel these cutthroats will take the bait," Rogers said, excitement in his voice.

"They can't pass up a chance like this," Fargo said. "Have everyone meet here Wednesday late afternoon. I'll spell out the details then."

"I'll contact everyone first thing in the morning," Rogers said, and strode into the house.

Fargo glanced at Isabel. "That was painless enough, wasn't it?" he asked.

"Yes," she said, and gave him a quick kiss, her lips soft sweetness, and hurried into the house.

Fargo stopped in at the kitchen, picked up some rabbit stew, and finally returned to the little corner room. He undressed and relaxed on the bed as he let his thoughts gather themselves. He had put things into motion. No more empty waiting.

He went over the details in his mind, again, as he listened to the ranch grow still, the last sounds from the bunkhouse drifting away. This was a relatively simple operation. The bait, the quarry, and the waiting hook. Still, details were important. They could spell success or failure, and he went over each item at least twice as he made a mental calendar of the order of things to come.

The night grew late and he was about to close his eyes when he heard the doorknob turn. He reached over and the big Colt was in his hand in a split second, aimed at the door as it slowly opened. "Christ," he swore as he saw the tall, willowy shape in the white silk nightgown. "That was a dumb thing to do," he hissed as he put the gun away.

"I suppose so," she admitted, and came to the bed. "I guess I was thinking about only one thing," she said as she wriggled her shoulders and the nightgown fell to her waist. The upturned full breasts thrust out at him, and her eyes flicked over his own muscled nakedness. She pushed the gown down over her hips, let it fall the rest of the way to the floor, and he took in the jet bush that curled its unruly fibers against her long thighs. He reached out, cupped his hands around both breasts, and she gave a tiny gasp of delight as she fell onto him. She stretched her body over his, pressed upon him, felt him rise under her, and uttered a long, groaning cry of pleasure.

He made love to her with hurried deliberation. Her long ebony hair flew wildly from side to side as she twisted and tossed her head, the flesh master of the spirit, all things consumed by the senses, until finally there were only the screams of ecstasy that trembled in the air as her body trembled against his.

When the stillness of exhaustion lay over the little room, she held herself against him. She slept until he woke her an hour before the dawn. "Yes," she said sleepily. "I know it's best." She sat up, pulled the nightgown on, and left the room with a glance back at him that held both smug pleasure and reproach.

He lay back and slept out the remainder of the night.

When morning came, he went about the first of the tasks he had put into order in his mind, and passed a row of brown-clad figures shuffling along as they gathered fox grapes. Father Junípero wasn't among the friars, he saw, and he rode on until he reached the mission. There, he saw another row of hooded friars pause as two wagons of laborers offered them melons.

Father Junípero emerged from the mission as Fargo rode up and dismounted. "Always a pleasure to have an unexpected visitor, my son," Father Junípero said from inside his brown hood. "But I fear I've nothing more to tell you."

"I've something to tell you," Fargo said. "It's about Father Malachy at Saint Mary's. He's decided to move that great cross to a safer place until all this raiding and killing is stopped."

"Perhaps a wise move," Father Junípero said.

"I want you to announce that during your Sunday services," Fargo said.

"In heaven's name, why? I'd think it should be kept secret," Father Junípero said.

"The exact night is a secret. But Father Malachy feels the people should know how concerned everyone is at these killings, even as far as Saint Mary's," Fargo said. "He feels it will make everyone more conscious of being careful, even those with little worth stealing."

"I see," Father Junípero said, his lips pursed. "That cross is a priceless object, with all those gems in it. Yet I am surprised they are moving it."

"It's the kind of thing this gang would go after. Father Malachy's being prudent. I told him I was sure you'd oblige him," Fargo said.

"Of course, of course."

"Thanks." Fargo smiled. "I'll be stopping by again." He turned the pinto and rode away at a slow trot. It had gone well. That part of the plan was in motion. Between Father Malachy's announcement at his Mass and the friars informing their parishioners, everyone in the whole damn area would know the precious cross was to be moved.

Fargo rode into the hills, scanned the land below as the day wore to a close, and he finally returned to the ranch just as Magdalena was about to drive off in her cart.

"I'm beginning to wonder if you are ever coming back, *mi amigo*," she said.

"In time. There are a lot of things going on now, a lot of plans to set into motion," he told her.

She nodded, happy to accept his answer. "I will be there," she said simply as she drove off.

He started toward the guest room when Isabel came from the house and he saw her black eyes narrowed at him.

"Remember when you accused me of being jealous?" she asked. "I denied it, but you were right. Only I didn't realize it then. I haven't stopped," she said, the message unsaid but unmistakable.

"I'll remember that," he said blandly, and she turned and strode into the house. He went to the guest room as night fell and made a wager with himself that he'd not have a visitor that night. He won, he reckoned as he pulled sleep around himself with a wry smile. She was still made of fire and ice.

# 6

Fargo's next step had to wait for dusk, and he relaxed during the day and watched Isabel work with the difficult Arabian. When she finished, she paused beside him, a tiny smile on her lovely lips. "Surprised last night?" she murmured.

"No."

"Damn you," she said, and then, a reluctant admission in her eyes, "I never knew self-discipline could be so hard."

"Self-discipline is good for the soul."

"And terrible on the body."

"I'm going to Saint Mary's now," he said. "I won't be back till late."

"I'll be in bed by then," she said.

He shrugged and strode into the house. He saddled the pinto and rode from the ranch as night began to slide over the land. A lone light burned inside a window at the church when he reached High River and he knocked at the tall, wooden door. It opened after a few moments and Father Malachy stared at him in surprise.

"I was just preparing my sermon for tomorrow," the priest said. "And my announcement."

"I've come to wrap," Fargo said. "You've any burlap here?"

"There are lots of old sacks downstairs," Father Malachy said, and stepped outside to lead Fargo around to the back of the church and a cellar door.

A lantern hung just inside the door and Father Malachy lighted it. Fargo found himself in a low-roofed room of thick stone walls. A jumble of things met his gaze—extra candlesticks, a ladder, a pile of burlap sacks, and against the fall wall, a half-dozen stone caskets. He spied the unfinished wooden cross, the arms attached but the wood still splintered and unpolished, the bottom with an extra piece also still attached.

"I'll be upstairs. Just close the cellar door when you're finished," Father Malachy said.

Fargo began to work, carefully wrapping the burlap sacks around the unfinished cross, tying each firmly in place. He worked carefully and slowly, and when he finished, the night had grown late. But he was satisfied. There was no way to know that the wrapped object was not the gem-encrusted cross. He placed a last cord around the bottom and walked from the dank, gloomy room, extinguished the lamp, and closed the cellar door.

Father Malachy answered his knock clad in a bathrobe.

"Finished," Fargo said. "I'll be back Wednesday evening. The men who'll be guarding the cross will be with me. I'll take them right to the cellar door. Nobody will see that the real cross is still in place inside the church."

"I'll be there," the priest said.

"I wish you'd reconsider and let me take the real cross," Fargo said. "I'd feel better about everythiing if I had hold of it, and it'd be safer, too."

"No, I'll not be reconsidering that," Father Malachy said firmly, and with a nod closed the tall door.

Fargo rode back along the road and took to the hills in a shortcut, but the last of the full moon was high in the sky when he returned to the ranch. He stabled the pinto and went to his small room, opened the door, and saw the willow-wand form atop the bed, beautifully naked and waiting.

She smiled at the surprise in his face as he closed the door. "I didn't say whose bed I'd be in," she murmured.

"True enough," he admitted as he shed clothes and slid himself against her.

She was warm, her mouth open and eager. She turned the night into a place of moaning ecstasy until she finally lay beside him, spent and satisfied. He woke her before the dawn once again and she rose with sleepy reluctance.

"I'll be going to Saint Mary's tomorrow with Father," she said, slipping a robe on.

"As you would any other Sunday," he said.

She nodded at the thinly veiled warning and melted into the darkness of the corridor outside. He returned to sleep. He stayed in bed until the others left for the trip to church, and then he rose, dressed, and rode almost in the tracks of the Brunswick. When he saw the tall spire of the church, he turned into the hills and followed the first passage that led upward. He stayed on the path, bore off at the first right, and explored the heavily wooded terrain that lined the paths. He marked each passage in his mind, and finally satisfied, he returned to the ranch as the day began to wind to an end.

Philip Rogers invited him to share the evening meal, and he carefully encouraged the man's excited anticipation without supplying any details. He saw the tiny smile touch Isabel's lips as she listened and watched. The meal ended, he returned to the room at the other end of the house and undressed, stretched out on the bed, and waited as the night grew late. Sermons had been given. Announcements made. The die was cast. And there were eyes already watching Saint Mary's, he was certain. When Isabel came into the room on silent, bare feet, she wore only a robe, which she tossed aside as she sat on the bed next to him.

"That was pretty fancy footwook during dinner," she remarked.

"Father Malachy, you, and me. No changes," he said, and she nodded.

"I want to be part of it Wednesday night," she said.

"No."

"Yes," she countered. "I'm into it. You brought me to see Father Malachy with you. I'm going to see it through."

"Your father won't allow it."

"I'll take care of Father. I always get my way," she said a trifle smugly. "Any more excuses?"

"One. You could get hurt, maybe killed," he said, and she slid arms around his neck and the pink-tipped breasts pressed into his chest.

"Thank you for caring," she murmured, and her lips found his, sweet wanting, until she pulled back. "Maybe nothing as exciting as this will ever happen in my life again. I'm not going to sit on the sidelines."

He hadn't time to answer as her mouth was on his again, pressing hard, her body sliding along his. There wasn't much point in talking, he decided, and he let wanting and the senses command the remainder of the night.

The next two days passed quickly. He rode the passages he had chosen again and again, made a mental chart through the thick blue spruce on the higher ground to the right, and finally Wednesday afternoon came and with it the other ranchers and their five men each.

Philip Rogers had picked his men, Alden Kirby among them, and he had supplied the wagon Fargo asked for: a one-horse farm wagon just large enough to hold the wooden cross.

Fargo faced the half-circle of waiting faces that gathered around him. It was time to spell out the working details, but no more than that.

"The wagon will carry the cross," he began. "Ten men will ride guard with the wagon. The rest of us will be out of sight in the heavy tree cover. We'll be riding parallel to you but on higher ground. They can't see us, or the whole thing will fail, but we'll be watching the wagon constantly."

"I'll pick the ten men for the wagon," Matt Stove said, and when he had finished, Fargo continued with his instructions.

"I'll go to the church with you to get the cross. You'll be on your own from there on. You take the first passage north into hill country, then cut east at the first side path. Stay on that path. You'll be in a hollow with heavy tree cover on both sides of you."

"Any idea where they might hit us?" Matt asked.

"No," Fargo answered. "But when they do, you dismount, take cover under and behind the wagon, and return their fire. They'll have to charge in to get the cross. As soon as they do, they'll come into the open and we'll open fire from the trees. I expect we might take the whole damn bunch of them in the first two volleys. We go after those left to run."

"Sounds foolproof," George Dodd said.

"Nothing's foolproof, but this is as good as I can make it. Let's ride," he said, and pulled himself onto the Ovaro.

Isabel and Philip Rogers rode alongside him until they drew near High River, where he halted in the new darkness of night.

"You wait here until I get back," he said to Rogers, and motioned to Matt Stove. The wagon rolled forward, the ten riders following, and Fargo hurried to join them.

It was a dark night, only the sliver of a new moon. He'd planned for that. There'd be almost no chance to pick up the riders who would move through the trees. When the tall steeple of the church became a black needle pointing skyward, he led the others to the cellar door.

Father Malachy came around from the front of the church as four men carried the burlap-wrapped cross from the crypt and put it into the wagon. He watched in silence until they were finished and Fargo was on the Ovaro again. "Godspeed," he said.

Fargo nodded back. "Thanks," he said, motioned to the others, and the wagon rumbled forward, the riders forming a line on each side. The Trailsman stayed with the group until the passage into the hills appeared. "I'll be leaving now," he said to Matt at the reins of the wagon. "East at the first side path. Keep on it until."

"Until," Stove said, and Fargo sent the Ovaro into a sharp turn and galloped into the dark night. Whoever had been watching the church had seen the cross loaded and the wagon roll away. He had raced away then, his orders to notify the others, who were waiting somewhere in the hills. Fargo rode into the blue spruce, turned north, and made his way to where he had left Isabel and the others.

"This way," he said, and found Isabel beside him as he lead the way to the high ground and the densely thick stand of spruce that paralleled the path below.

He halted, waited, and finally saw the wagon and its guards come into sight below. Slowly, he started forward, keeping pace with the wagon, and motioned for the others to ride in silence. The passage below held few turns as it moved up and down through the hilly terrain. The riders and wagon disappeared from sight only when the tree cover grew unusually thick.

Fargo guessed they had been riding close to an hour when the silent black night shattered with a burst of gunfire from the trees on the other side of the path below. He yanked the Ovaro to a halt, his eyes on the men as they dived from their horses. Some scrambled under the wagon while others took cover behind it.

They began to return fire, shots sent aimlessly into the trees in the general direction of the unseen attackers. The fusillade from the trees escalated, slacked off, then increased in fury again. They were firing in volleys, one after the other, a steady drumfire of bullets. Fargo felt the restlessness of the men around him. "Easy," he warned. "They'll show. Then we hit them." But as the gunfire from the distant trees continued in cascading fusillades, the men by the wagon were kept pinned down. Finally he heard Philip Rogers' words. "They're not coming down," Rogers said.

"They can't get the cross by just shooting at it. They've got to come down," Fargo said, and frowned at the scene below. The gunfire refused to let up, and he felt the frown dig deeper into his brow. "Dammit, what are they waiting for?" he bit out.

"Maybe to kill everyone with the wagon first," Isabel said.

"Not from up there. Everybody's too well hunkered down. They can see that," Fargo said. "Goddamn, why haven't they come after the cross?" Mockingly, another volley of shots exploded from the trees to

slam into the wagon and then, with startling sudden-
ness, the gunfire trailed off. Another sound followed,
the unmistakable clatter of horses starting to race
through thick mountain brush.

"Goddamn, they're running. They're giving up.
After them," Philip Rogers shouted, and sent his
mount racing down toward the path below and the hill
of trees on the other side.

The others charged after him, all except Fargo. He
stared into space as he listened to the sound of the
fleeing attackers, already high into hills. He saw the
men with the wagon leap onto their horses and follow
Philip Rogers as he swept past them.

"Dammit," Fargo bit out. "Dammit to hell." His
lips pulled back in a grimace of frustration and fury
as he yanked the Ovaro around and raced off through
the trees. He flung curses into the wind as he skirted
tree trunks at a full gallop. He heard the sound of a
horse following and threw a glance backward, to see
Isabel. He hadn't time to slow for explanations and
kept his headlong pace. The Arabian wasn't fast
enough to catch up to him, but it was fast enough to
stay on his tail as he barreled out of the trees and
down onto flat land, a racing, cursing specter in the
dark of the nearer moonless night.

Isabel's horse had slowed to fall a dozen strides
behind him when Fargo saw the spire of Saint Mary's.
He continued to charge on until he reached the church
and leapt from the saddle before the pinto had come
to a halt. The tall front door of the church was open,
lamplight glowing from inside, and he halted at the
door as Isabel charged to a halt and swung to the
ground. He waited for her, and when she reached
him, he stepped into the church and stumbled over
the figure in a black cassock that lay just inside the
vestibule. He turned the figure over as he cursed

inwardly and looked down at a thin-faced man with brown hair and a bullet hole in his chest.

"My God, it's Williams, the sacristan," Isabel said and followed Fargo as he rose, moved quickly into the nave of the church. His eyes instantly went to the rear wall. It was empty, a faint outline where the cross had hung. He ran down the center aisle of the church, circled behind the altar, and cursed as he skidded to a halt. The cross lay on the floor, looking pockmarked where each precious gem had been gouged from it. Near the left arm of the cross the figure of Father Malachy lay slumped against the back of the altar, three bullet holes seeping red onto the black cassock.

"Oh, God," Isabel breathed. "Oh, God."

"This is why they didn't attack the wagon," Fargo said, his voice strained. "This is why they just kept everybody pinned down and waiting. They were buying time for the ones who came here."

"How did they know?" Isabel murmured.

"They didn't. They outfoxed me, damn their stinking souls," Fargo said. "I underestimated them, dammit." He swore silently as he gazed down at the slumped figure of Father Malachy. "If he'd let me move the cross, he'd be alive now. They'd have come, seen the cross was gone, and left," he said angrily.

"Maybe Father and the others caught them."

"Not a chance on a night like this, not with the start they had. They scattered and disappeared into the darkness."

"There's an undertaker in town, Ed Blayley. I'll get him," Isabel volunteered, and he nodded and watched her hurry away.

He leaned against the wall and let the bitter anger churn inside him. Substitute plans, he bit out in silent anger. They failed more often than not. He stayed with the frustration and sorrow swirling through him, and finally Isabel returned with two men who had plainly thrown on clothes. They stared at the scene and blessed themselves.

"We'll take care of everything, Miss Rogers," the one said.

"Father will come over in the morning," she said, and the two men nodded as they moved toward Father Malachy. She turned and Fargo followed her out of the church. "There's a provincial house up north at Cape Mendocino. Father will arrange to get a message to them. It'll take days, of course," Isabel said as they rode from the church.

Fargo nodded, but the bitterness still held him. "My damn fault," he said. "I didn't think it through far enough. I didn't expect they'd be that smart."

"Mistakes happen. Sometimes you misjudge. As you said, Father Malachy would be alive if he'd let you take the cross in the first place."

"Yes, but the bottom line is I set a trap and they sprung it back on me," he muttered darkly. "It won't happen again."

He fell silent and she let him ride with his dark and angry thoughts. When they reached the ranch, he found that Rogers had returned only a few minutes earlier. The grimness in his face made the obvious question unnecessary. Isabel spoke first, quickly recounting what they had found at Saint Mary's, and when she finished, Rogers frowned in shock. "Good God," he murmured first, and then stared at his daughter. "You knew about this? You knew we were riding guard on a substitute cross?"

"Yes," she said. "Only three of us knew, Fargo, Father Malachy, and myself. We agreed it was safest to keep it that way."

"You satisfied now, Fargo?" Alden Kirby cut in.

"About what?"

"That it has to be the damn villagers. The managers and foremen of every ranch were with us," Kirby said triumphantly.

"And any of them could have set it up before joining us," Fargo said. "These bastards are being too clever to be a bunch of villagers. They're professionals, or somebody damn smart is calling the shots."

Kirby uttered a derisive sound as he strode away and Fargo met Philip Rogers' frown. "Whatever the answer is, we're getting nowhere, Fargo," the man said, and Fargo found the frustration and reproach in his tone all too understandable. "What, now?" Rogers demanded.

"You set a trap that doesn't work, you set another," Fargo answered, and Philip Rogers nodded grimly as he walked into the house.

"Father's upset. I guess we all are, especially over Father Malachy," Isabel said.

"I'm not exactly happy," he said, and she pressed her lips to his cheek before following her father inside.

Fargo unsaddled the Ovaro, stabled and fed the horse, and went to the little corner room. He undressed and stretched out on the bed. Only one thing was certain in his mind: there'd be no more waiting. He'd search and probe and dig. He'd find a way to bring them out again, even if it meant making himself the bait. And he'd investigate the villages. Not because he'd come around to agreeing with Alden Kirby but because he could no longer, in conscience, overlook anything or anyone.

Isabel did not appear, nor did he expect her. It was a night for grieving. He fell asleep to wake only when the sun streamed through the two windows.

He rose, quickly washed and dressed, and hurried to the stable. He saddled the pinto and rode from the ranch just as Isabel stepped from the house. He waved back at her and rode on, turned west, and took the path toward High River. A visit to Saint Mary's was first on his list of things to do. He'd comb every inch of the church and the grounds around it. Maybe he'd find something. He'd take anything that might turn into a lead.

He kept the pinto at a steady pace, crossed a low hill, and came down on the other side, where the land flattened into the road toward town. He was nearly at High River when he slowed, a frown of surprise sliding across his face as he saw the lone, brown-robed figure with the white cincture at the waist, the hood pulled up against the heat of the sun.

He drew to a halt when he reached the figure, and the man stopped, pushed the hood back with one hand, and peered up at him. Fargo saw a round-cheeked, ruddy face, one he didn't recognize, but then he knew hardly a handful of the friars by sight, he reminded himself.

" 'Morning," he called out. "Are you from the mission?"

"The Mission of Santa Angelica?" the monk asked.

"That's the one."

"No, I'm not from the mission, but I'm on my way there."

"To become part of the mission?" Fargo questioned.

"No, I'm on my yearly pilgrimage to all the missions in the state for the provincialate. Santa Angelica is my last stop. The order has me visit each mission to see if anything is needed, though each mission is expected to be self-sufficient," the friar said. "I'm Brother Rolando."

"Well, Brother, you'll find they've had more than their share of troubles at the mission," Fargo said. "Are you expected?"

"Oh, yes. A letter was sent some three months ago,

**113**

informing the good brothers I'd be arriving sometime this week," Brother Rolando said, a smile wreathing his round-cheeked, ruddy face. "I have learned over the years of traveling by foot that I can be fairly precise about time."

"I'm wordering if I ought to ride along with you," Fargo said. "The mission has had its own troubles, but this whole region has become real dangerous. A gang of cutthroat killers is operating here."

Brother Rolando smiled benignly. "Thank you for the offer, my friend, but I will be quite safe. We friars travel the world over because everyone knows we carry neither coins, nor gold, nor any other valuables. What need is there to attack such a traveler, I ask you?"

"None," Fargo conceded. "But I'd be careful nevertheless. The world is full of vicious people."

"I'll be quite safe, but I thank you again," Brother Rolando said. "Godspeed to you, my son." With a flip of one hand he brought the hood back over his head and walked on with a brisk and confident step.

Fargo watched the prints of his sandaled feet in the dust of the road for a moment before he turned the Ovaro and rode on to Saint Mary's, where he dismounted and moved into the church through the still-open door. He walked slowly down the nave, his eyes sweeping the floor, peering under pews, until he halted at the altar. He walked around both sides and then examined the floor behind the altar as he carefully went over the pockmarked cross, which still lay at an angle against the rear wall. The gems had been gouged out with a knife, he concluded, perhaps two knives, two men working together on each one.

Finally he went outside and began to scan the ground in methodical fashion. Five horses, he decided as he found where the raiders had raced off into the brush-covered land behind the church. Nothing distinctive on the hoofprints, he noted unhappily. When he finished searching the ground around the church, he swung onto the pinto and followed the hoofprints to where they went into the mountain brush. But as he expected, the prints quickly became all but impossible to track, as they were all but obliterated by the thick, wiry mountain brush.

Fargo tried following one set where the brush was still pressed down into the earth, but he soon came to a wide and fast-running mountain stream. There were no signs of hoofprints on the other side, he noted grimly. This particular horseman had taken to the stream to make his escape in one direction or the other. The others had scattered on their own.

Fargo, tight-lipped, turned back to Saint Mary's for a long, last look, and rode away, not surprised at having found nothing. Besides being ruthless, the bandits were clever and careful. But they had good horses, sturdy enough for hard, fast mountain riding. It was unlikely they'd be using any of the Arabians from the ranches. But his thoughts went to the brothers at the mission and the mounts they kept to sell. Maybe they had sold some within the last few months. If so, they'd perhaps remember to whom. It was worth following up, he decided, and he turned the pinto back toward the hill country where the mission nestled.

He rode a low hill that led to the Rogers' ranch and down onto the narrow pathway on the other side. A smile edged his lips as he picked up the distinctive, sandaled footprints of Brother Rolando along the dusty path. He had just moved over the top of a shallow rise in the path when he saw the brown-robed figure. But not striding briskly along the path. Brother Rolando lay prone, facedown on the ground, the brown robe and hood shroudlike over him.

Fargo spurred the Ovaro forward and leapt from the saddle as he reached the friar. He knelt down on one knee and carefully turned the man onto his back. Brother Rolando was dead. A single bullet through the coarse brown material left a red stain across his chest.

The Trailsman swore softly as his eyes went to the roadway at once. There were no footprints and no hoofmarks. The friar had been shot from a distance. As he stared at the inert figure in the brown robe he recalled Brother Rolando's own words: "Everyone knows we carry neither gold, nor coins, nor any other valuables. What need is there to attack such a traveler?" What need, indeed? Fargo frowned. Unless the friar had come upon something. Unless, like Magdalena's uncle, he had seen something he wasn't supposed to see. Something or someone.

"Damn," Fargo swore aloud as he lifted the friar and laid him across the saddle on his stomach. Now he had another reason to visit the mission. He hoped no others would be this sour as he slowly rode on, his eyes sweeping the terrain on both sides. But only the cowbirds and scarlet tanagers moved the leaves in the thick stands of gambel oak and hawthorn.

Fargo finally reached the mission. As he rode into the courtyard, he saw Father Junípero come out to greet him while a half-dozen other friars moved in silent pairs along the stone-walled corridors. They halted to stare at him as he swung from the Ovaro. "Fargo, what is this?" Father Junípero frowned.

"This is Brother Rolando. He told me earlier that he was on his way here," Fargo said.

"Brother Rolando," the priest said, frowning. "Yes, of course, from the provincialate. He was making his yearly round of visits to the missions. We had received a letter about his arrival. And he's been killed? Oh, my Lord, my Lord."

"Shot. Murdered," Fargo said, and Father Junípero stared back in shock.

"After what happened to Father Malachy at Saint Mary's," he said. "Word reached us this morning. What is going on here? What terrible evil holds this land?"

"That's what I aim to find out," Fargo said.

Father Junípero turned to the friars who were looking on. "Come, take Brother Rolando into the chapel," he said, and Fargo stepped back as four of the friars lifted the figure from the saddle and carried it into the mission. Other friars appeared and Father Junípero motioned them all into the chapel. "Prayers at once, at once," he said. As still other friars appeared to hurry into the mission, heads bowed under their hoods, he turned back to Fargo.

"I was on my way here when I came onto him," Fargo said. "I'm sorry to bother you at a time like this, but I want to ask about your horses."

"Our horses?"

"The ones you sell," Fargo said, and started to walk to where the horses were tethered. "They've just been washed down," he said as he saw their still-wet coats.

"Yes, the brothers groom them every week. A clean animal is a contented and healthy animal, we feel," Father Junípero said.

"Can't argue with that."

"Besides, you never know when a buyer will show up. We like to keep the horses in good condition."

"I came to talk about buyers. Who was your last one?" Fargo asked.

The priest frowned in thought. "A man who appeared with a companion," he said after a moment.

"When?"

"About three months back. We don't keep records. He bought six of our horses."

"Six?"

"Yes, we were all quite overjoyed about our windfall," Father Junípero said.

"I'm sure you were. Can you describe the man?" Fargo queried.

"Tall, with a large nose. Black hair. He carried a gun, of course."

"He say where he was from or where he was taking the horses?" Fargo pressed.

"No, nothing at all."

"Is he still around? Have any of the brothers seen him again?"

"No. Why? What is this all about?"

"I think your horses may be being used by these *bandidos*," Fargo said, and saw Father Junípero's lined face grow longer in shock.

"What a terrible thought," the *padre* murmured.

"It's a maybe," Fargo said gently, though he felt it was very much a probability.

"It's too much for me to think about now. I must go inside and join the others. We will give Brother Rolando a proper burial. Be assured of that," Father Junípero said. "Afterward, I will send a message to the provincialate. Perhaps I'll have one of the brothers deliver it himself." He turned and hurried into the chapel as Fargo rode from the mission courtyard.

The villages were next on the agenda the Trailsman had set for himself, and he started with the one on the hill behind Magdalena's place. He let the Ovaro amble among the collection of small, square whitewashed houses, but he saw mostly burros with but a few quarter horses that were well past their mountain-riding abilities. He went on to the next village and found more of the same. The one after that was little different.

It was only when he reached the last of the villages in the region that he spotted two good-looking brown horses tethered loosely behind a flat-roofed house. He dismounted as his practiced eye took in their sturdy legs, deep chests, and sound hindquarters.

A man came around the corner of the house. He was small of build and had a drooping mustache; he wore white trousers and a long white shirt that hung almost to his knees.

"You like the horses, *señor*?" he asked.

"Seem real nice," Fargo said.

"I rent them," the man said, and Fargo felt the twinge of excitement push at him.

"To anybody?" he questioned.

"Depends. I have two customers who use them every week or so," the man said, and the twinge stabbed harder inside Fargo.

"You know what they use the horses for?" he asked, and expected the man to say he didn't.

"*Sí, señor*. They use them to let little children ride on them," the man said.

"These horses?" Fargo frowned, disbelief in his voice. The man untied one and used the loose tether to run the horse a half-dozen times in a wide circle. When he brought the animal to a halt, Fargo heard the deep, wheezing sound as the horse blew air, a sound that meant only one thing. "His lungs are shot," he said, and frowned.

"The other one is the same," the man said. "They were very sick once, I was told. That's why I got them for nothing."

"Probably had pneumonia from not being dried out after a run and left in a drafty stable," Fargo said. "It kills most horses." He swore silently as he turned away, the excitement inside him shattered as a balloon bursts. He had seen mounts such as these two before, the kind that looked good at first sight.

He nodded at the man and rode away wrapped in frustration as one more lead dissipated. He circled back the way he had come and it was dusk when he stopped in at Magdalena's place.

She greeted him with warm hugs, and he had coffee with her. She wanted to have more, but he made an excuse to leave. Isabel would be waiting for him to return, he knew. If he didn't, that intuitive sharpness of hers would supply the reason, and this was not a time to complicate things further.

The tiredness of frustration was still wrapped around him when he reached the Rogers' place. He spoke to Philip Rogers and Isabel inside the house. He told them about Brother Rolando, and when he finished, he found Rogers clung to a grim optimism. "A few minutes earlier and you'd have been there to see whatever it was the friar did," Rogers said.

"That's the way it's all been. Luck, timing, everything in their favor, everything just out of our reach," Fargo said.

"But it shows they're out there. They'll make a mistake," Rogers said.

"We can't wait for that, dammit," Fargo bit out. "I've got to find another way to bring them into the open."

"Stay with it," Rogers said, and Isabel walked outside with Fargo.

"I'll come by later," she said.

"I won't be there," he told her. "Your father's right. They're out there. I'm going to be, too. Maybe I'll get lucky."

"Everyone will be going to Mass at the mission

tomorrow," she said. "Saint Mary's is closed down until another priest is sent. Will I see you there?"

"I'll stop in."

She reached up and her lips were softly warm against his. "So you don't forget."

"I don't figure to do that," he said, and she watched as he climbed onto the Ovaro and rode into the night. He went to the ledge that let him see in all directions. The moon had grown fuller, enough so to throw a silver patina over the land. He settled down against the trunk of a spruce and relaxed as the night sounds drifted up to him. But as the night grew long, he felt the frustration catch hold of him again. Nothing he watched for moved across the countryside below, and it was only when the night neared an end that he let himself sleep into the warmth of the morning sun.

# 7

The Mass had just ended when he arrived at the mission. He had washed in a mountain stream, dressed, and ridden leisurely down out of the hills. He had been in no mood for hurrying, the dark shroud of frustration still around him. But he smiled as he saw the number of carriages outside the mission walls—a first for Mass at the mission, he was certain. He watched the villagers walk past the fancy carriages in small clusters, hurrying on their way, the women still with shawls on their heads. Some mounted their small burros but most left on foot.

He moved forward as he spied Isabel hurrying toward a Basket phaeton.

She saw him as she climbed into the carriage and waited till he drew alongside. "Father came with the Stoves in their surrey. Ride with me," she said, and he tied the Ovaro's reins to the back of the carriage and slid into the single seat beside her. She snapped the reins lightly and the horse moved forward at once. "Nothing happened last night, I take it," she said crisply.

"Nothing," he said, and caught the irritation in her manner. "Something digging at you?"

"The Mass," she snapped. "It was almost disgraceful."

"Maybe you're just used to bigger and fancier," he commented.

"I'm used to things being done correctly," she shot back with annoyance. "I expected it would be a low Mass, but I didn't expect it would be so miserably conducted."

"Such as?" he inquired as she steered the phaeton past a cluster of villagers.

"I've never heard Latin spoken so atrociously, with so many mispronunciations. I didn't expect the beauty of the Jesuit-schooled Latin, but that Father Junípero was disgraceful. I've heard first-grade students read better than that. I could barely understand a word," Isabel said.

"I guess some folks are no good at Latin, priest or not," Fargo offered, but she wasn't to be placated.

"He should've been better than what I heard," she snapped. "Maybe the villagers who go there don't know any different and don't expect any better. I can understand that. I can even forgive his atrocious Latin, but I can't forgive the other things in the ceremony."

"The other things?" Fargo echoed.

"Parts of the ritual I just don't understand how they could ignore. They had the chalice standing on the bare stone of the altar. There should've been a corporal under it. Then there was no purificator over the chalice and no pall covering the host. He wore the maniple on his left arm instead of his right. One of the friars acted as server. After the reading from the missal, the server takes the book from the epistle side of the altar to the gospel side. They just left it where it was. Half the time he didn't bother to genuflect when he should have, and he didn't kiss the gospel after he'd finished reading from it."

"Seems you're a real hard critic," Fargo said.

"No, these things are basic to the ritual of the Mass. They are Franciscans, members of the Church. They ought to conduct a proper Mass at least. I won't be going back," she said with icy disapproval as they drove under the iron arch and she drew up in front of the house.

Fargo untied the Ovaro and one of the hands took the carriage away.

"Where are you going?" Isabel asked as he climbed into the saddle.

"I'm going to search the hill country where they took off after they had the wagon pinned down. I expect it'll be another wild-goose chase, but I'm getting used to that."

She nodded and watched him ride away.

He put the pinto into a trot, turned west after he left the ranch, and found his way back to where the wagon had been pinned down. A frown had ridden with him as he'd thought about how barbed Isabel had been about the service at the mission. He felt strangely disturbed at her reactions. Arrogant and disdainful were but two words that fit her attitude. He was bothered. It seemed an abrupt return to the Isabel he'd first met. Perhaps she'd never really left, he mused. Perhaps the warm young woman who'd suddenly shown understanding and a new compassion had been a passing moment. Years of aristocratic pride and disdain didn't disappear overnight, he realized, yet he felt bothered and saddened by the reversal. He thought about all the things she'd said. There'd been no understanding or leniency, no sparing of any kind, only icy condemnation. Fire and ice, he grunted. The words still fit.

He pushed further thoughts of Isabel's anger from his mind as he concentrated on his search. Finding hoofprints was out of the question, he knew, and he searched the thick brush and heavy tree cover for some piece of physical evidence, a torn patch of shirt, a spur that had come loose and fallen to the ground, perhaps a hat lost in flight, a piece of boot heel, anything that might serve as a concrete lead.

But the day wore on toward an end and Fargo found nothing as he crisscrossed the hills for the final time. He turned and rode downward to the path that led from High River and halted when he reached the spot where he had found Brother Rolando's body. His lips pulled back in a grimace as he swept the land that surrounded the spot. What could the friar have come upon here in broad daylight in this lonely road? Magdalena's uncle had been killed for what he had seen, but he hadn't been in the mountains on a lonesome road.

Both men slain for something they'd come upon. It fitted yet it didn't fit. Fargo frowned as he rode on through the dusk. His thoughts continued to swirl through his mind as night fell and he returned to the ranch.

He managed to get something to eat in the kitchen, though the ranch was still and dark. He went to the corner room, undressed, and lay across the bed, aware that he was still bothered by the way that day had turned. Isabel's attitude toward the Mass at the mission, her accusations, Brother Rolando's death on the mountain roadway, things that didn't hang together yet kept pushing at one another. He was frowning into the dark when the door opened and Isabel slipped into the room clothed in a white robe. She sat down at the edge of the bed and the moonlight let him see the faint smile on her lips.

"You're annoyed with me, aren't you?" she said, and he realized that astonishment flooded his face as he sat up on one elbow.

"Don't know if that's exactly right," he returned.

"Close enough," she said, and his shrug was an admission. "I felt it when you rode off this morning," she added, and he let a wry smile edge his lips as he marveled at the acuity of her intuition. "We can talk about it. Later," she said, and took off the robe from her and let him stare at the full-cupped willowy beauty that was here. She came forward, pushed herself over him, the pale-pink tips of her breasts already firm, and there was a wild haste in her wanting that was not unlike a consuming flame. He felt it in her touch, in her guttural half-sob, in her body as she slid her legs up and down across his groin and he came afire with her. In moments the little room echoed to the sounds of flesh meeting flesh, the mingling of bodies and senses until, finally, all the ecstasy spiraled into oneness and his groan matched her half-screamed sob.

She lay still and warm against him for minutes that were made of satiated silence, then she moved, rose, and sat up, her thighs resting against his legs. "Talk to me. You said you didn't know if 'annoyed' was the right word. What is the right word?" she asked, and waited.

He realized he was staring at her as suddenly thoughts leapt crazily in his mind and he felt the wave of excitement stab at him. All the things that hadn't hung together suddenly pushed against one another in a strange mixture that made a grim, distasteful kind of sense. "I was all wrong," he said, and Isabel frowned back. "I thought I was bothered by your attitude toward the friars and their Mass. Then it was what Brother Rolando could have seen at midday on a lonely mountain path."

"I'm not following you," Isabel said.

"It wasn't your attitude. It was the things you said, that catalog of mistakes and accusations. They kept sticking into me," Fargo told her. "And then maybe he didn't see anything at all. It all just sorted itself out."

"I'm still lost," Isabel said.

"Brother Rolando. Maybe he didn't see anything at all. Maybe he was shot to keep him from reaching the mission," Fargo said, and watched her eyes grow wide. "You said the Mass was so wrong in so many places. You said you couldn't understand why. Maybe the reason is the same for Brother Rolando and the Mass," he went on.

Isabel sat up straight and looked breathtakingly lovely even as the horrified shock slid into her face. "Father Junípero?" she gasped.

"I don't know." Fargo shrugged. "But I know that his story about arriving and finding all the brothers dead or near dead of food poisoning is all his. Nobody was there. Nobody knows what happened."

"Are you saying you think he made all that up?"

"Can you say he didn't? Can you say he did?" Fargo tossed back at her. "I can't say either way because I sure as hell don't know. Neither does anybody else."

Isabel frowned at him. "The villagers that go to the mission believed the story. So did we all when we heard it."

"Sure. It's a perfectly plausible story, perfectly believable. There was no reason not to believe it," Fargo said.

"Until now."

"Until now," he echoed.

"What about Magdalena's uncle? You were sure he

was killed for something he saw. Are you changing that, too?"

"No, I'm staying with that. But I made the same assumption about Brother Rolando, and that may have been a mistake," Fargo said.

"What made you suddenly doubt Brother Rolando was killed for something he saw?"

"Pedro was near the mission, maybe at it, before he ran for his life. Brother Rolando was walking down a mountain path in the middle of the day. What could he have seen there?"

"You never know."

"No, there's always the possibility, but it's getting slimmer every time I think about it," he said.

"What else?"

"Little things. Always pay attention to the little things." Fargo smiled grimly. "The villagers have gone to Mass there every week. Maybe they noticed some changes. Maybe they didn't. The thing is that they wouldn't question anything. Acceptance is bred into them. It's part of their life to accept things the way they are. They're used to taking the cards life deals them."

"I suppose so."

"The good friars are the church. The villagers would never question men of God. They're too deeply faithful for that."

"Are you saying I lack faith?" Isabel answered with just the hint of defensiveness.

"I'm saying you were brought up not to accept anything," he said. " 'Cept one thing."

"What's that?"

"Being queen bee," he returned.

"Bastard," she said, but couldn't suppress a smile. "You've just got more questions now."

"I figure to get some answers."

"How?"

"The friars who died of food poisoning are all in the newest graves atop the hill behind the mission. I'm going to do some digging," Fargo said.

Isabel's face darkened in shocked distaste. "You're not," she breathed.

"As soon as I get a shovel, a lantern, and the right time," he said grimly.

"When will that be?"

"Tomorrow night, I'd guess. I saw the signs this afternoon. Rain is on the way."

"Why is rain important?"

"It'll make for a dark night. Everybody will stay inside the mission and it'll make the ground soft," Fargo said.

"What do you expect to prove?"

"Maybe nothing. Maybe a lot."

She thought for a moment. "You'll need somebody to help, hold the lantern."

"Magdalena will go with me. She has a stake in this."

"We all have a stake in it," Isabel countered.

"She has a special stake. It was her uncle who was killed." '

Isabel's frown deepened. "You think the bandits and this are tied together?"

"I don't know." Fargo shrugged. "But I'm going to find out."

Magdalena won't help you," Isabel said flatly.

"Of course she will," Fargo said, and received a slightly chiding smile along with a kiss. Isabel slipped from the room and he lay back and frowned as he let sleep sweep him into its arms.

When morning came, he took a stout shovel and a kerosene lantern from the supply shed, put them in his room, and watched with satisfaction as the sky turned gray. By afternoon, the rain had come, a strong, steady downpour. He got out his rain slicker at the day's end and climbed onto the Ovaro. He had to pass the ranch on the way back to the mission, and he left the shovel and lantern in the room to pick up later.

The rain was steady and the night pitch-black when he reached Magdalena's place, and she was both surprised and happy to see him. Isabel's remark had stayed in his thoughts and he decided not to face Magdalena with the possible enormity of what had become very definite suspicions.

"I need your help, Magdalena," he said. "You know the mission graveyard atop the hill. I have to go there."

"Go there?" She frowned. "On a night like this?"

"I have to open a few of the graves," he said. "Just to be sure of something."

He saw the horror slide across her round-cheeked face. "Open the graves?" she gasped. "No, no. You cannot do that."

"I have to," he said gently. "I have to satisfy myself about something. I need you to hold the lantern."

The horror deepened in her face. "No, no, never. That is desecration. That is a terrible sin. You cannot do that. You will be cursed forever," she said, and he saw the fear and horror in her face was too deep for words to change or reason to reach.

"Maybe you're right," he said, and she closed her arms around him and clung tightly.

"It would not be right, *mi amigo*. It would be bad," she said, and he held her close and stroked her thick black curls. "What would make you want to do such a terrible thing," she asked.

He half-shrugged, aware that to tell her his suspicions would run head-on into the deepest roots of her beliefs. She'd reject the very thought and perhaps him with it, and he didn't want that. Magdalena had knowledge he might still need. But her deep black eyes were on him, waiting for an answer, and his thoughts raced desperately. "Something I heard," he said. He knew he sounded lame, but it gave him another few precious seconds to find a reason that would satisfy her.

"What?" Magdalena frowned.

"Brother Julio befriended one of the *bandidos* once, without knowing who he was," Fargo began. "The man gave Brother Julio a ring with his name on it. I thought if the brother had died wearing the ring, I could find it."

"And the *bandido's* name would be on it," Magdalena finished.

"Exactly," he said, and held the sigh of relief inside himself.

"There is no excuse for the desecration of the dead. Not even such a one. The dead take their secrets with them. That is the way it is meant to be," Magdalena said.

He nodded and let himself appear chastened. "It was a thought," he murmured, and she clung to him once more.

"A sinful thought," she said, and then lifted her head to his. "When will you stay the night again?"

"Soon," he said, and she was content with a long kiss. She watched him vanish into the rain-swept night from the door and he rode carefully through the inky blackness.

The ground had already softened under the pinto's hooves, and the rain continued in a steady downpour as Fargo reached the ranch. He frowned as he saw the gray Arabian outside the corner of the house. He started to dismount when the figure appeared clad in a deep-blue oilskin outfit. Isabel peered up at him from under the wide brim of the rain hat and he saw the shovel and lantern in her hands.

"I don't see anyone with you," she said tartly.

"Don't be a smart-ass," he growled, and took the lantern and shovel from her as she climbed onto the Arabian. He kept the shovel and handed the lantern back to her as she rode from the ranch beside him. "How come you will come with me?" he slid at her.

"Faith is different things to different people. Some have to believe without question. Others have to question to believe," she answered.

"How'd you get to be so wise so young?"

"Flattery will get you anywhere," she said. "Though it seems you've done quite all right without it."

A gust of rain slammed down hard to toss away an answer, not that he had one, and he lowered his head against the storm. He felt the hill rising under him, though he could see precious little. It was only when a flash of lightning broke apart the blackness that he saw the mission just below and to his left. It was enough to let him regain his bearings, and he headed downward as he went north. Another lightning flash let him see that he was almost upon the hill with the rows of crosses dotting the top section. He reined to a halt and dismounted.

"We walk from here," he said. "Let's light the lantern."

With Isabel holding the lantern and his back shielding it from the rain, he managed to get it lit. The soft yellow glow spread just far enough for him to make out the first row of crosses. Isabel held the lantern low to the ground, where it afforded them the most amount of light while they walked to the top of the hill.

Fargo halted at the newest double row of crosses,

the wood not yet weathered by years of sun and rain. He raised the lantern to peer at the name scrawled at the bottom of each cross, and finally halted. "Father Antonio," he said. "We start here."

Isabel set the lantern on the ground but held on to it as he took the shovel and began to dig. The rain-soaked ground made the task much easier, he realized gratefully as he lifted the muddy earth into a pile at one side. But it was still slow work before he had the simple pine box uncovered. He paused to glance at Isabel. "Maybe you'd like to wait over there," he suggested. "This is going to be rough."

"I'll stay here. We don't want the lantern to slip and fall in this muddy ground," she said.

He nodded, lowered himself on both knees, and reached down with the edge of the shovel, sliding the implement along the top edge of the coffin until he found a spot to wedge the edge upward. He worked carefully, felt the lid of the box begin to lift, and his lips pulled back in distaste. He didn't want to feel like a ghoul, yet that was exactly how he felt. He swore at himself as the one end of the lid came loose. He moved to the other end and pried that loose in but a few moments more.

"More light," he muttered, and Isabel stepped closer and raised the lantern. He reached down with both hands and pulled the lid of the box up to stare down at the mostly decomposed remains of the body. He saw Isabel look away as he used the handle end of the shovel to poke about.

The rain pelted into the coffin and Fargo steeled himself against the odor that began to drift upward as he pushed against the remains with the shovel handle. "Goddamn," he swore finally, and pushed himself backward to rest on his knees at the edge of the grave. He was breathing hard, he realized, and felt a dirtiness that was more inner than outer. He raised his eyes to meet Isabel's stare.

"No damn food poisoning," he said, and she stared back unblinkingly. "There's a bullet hole smack in the middle of his forehead," he finished, and heard her small gasp. He rose, anger part of his grimness now, replaced the lid on the box, and began to furiously shovel the grave closed.

"Next," he spit out when he'd finished.

"Isn't one enough?" Isabel asked.

"No," he said, more roughly than he'd intended, and she fell silent as he began to dig up the next grave. He forced himself not to hurry as his shoulder muscles began to ache, and when he had the grave open, he again used the shovel to pry up the lid of the coffin. He leaned down into the grave, holding the lantern himself this time, and there was no hole in the skull. He frowned and slowly moved the lantern; he suddenly halted and stared down at the breastplate of the skeleton. The center was shattered, along with the ends of two ribs, plainly the result of two shots through the chest.

Once again he shoved dirt back until the grave was closed. Ignoring Isabel's protest, he dug up still another grave, and this time found that the base of the skull inside the coffin had been shattered. "Three. That'll do," he grunted as he shoveled the grave closed.

By the time he had finished, dawn waited just over the mountain peaks. He turned the lantern off as he made his way back to the horses, with Isabel clinging to his arm. She rode back in silence, wrapped in her own thoughts as he was in his.

The rain stopped when they reached the ranch and she came to the room with him, shed the wet oilskins and the clothes beneath, and stretched out on the bed with him.

He felt the shudder run through her as she clung to him. "You did real well," he told her.

"I feel dirty inside," she said.

"I know."

"I know what we found. I don't know what we proved. I don't know what it all means," she said.

"I don't either. But three of the last friars here didn't die of food poisoning. They were shot to death. I'll bet that holds for all the rest of them."

"But how does this tie in with the bandits?" Isabel frowned.

"I don't know yet."

"You think these friars have somehow been working with them?" she suggested.

"It's possible," Fargo said. "That'd make these friars something less than holy men."

"What if we stumbled onto something terrible here that has nothing to do with the bandits?" Isabel asked.

"I thought about that, too," Fargo said. "It's possible. It seems damn near anything is possible right now."

"What next?" she asked. "Where do we go from here?"

"I'm thinking about laying it out in front of Father Junípero," Fargo said. "I want to see what happens."

"Do you think that would be wise, given all the possibilities involved?" Isabel questioned.

"I'm not interested in wise. I'm interested in rocking the boat, any which way it goes."

"Are you going to tell Father what we found tonight?"

He thought for a moment. "Not now, not till we know more. Too many things have gone sour," he said, and saw her accept his decision without protest.

"When are you going to confront Father Junípero?" she asked.

"After I get a couple hours' sleep," he said.

She nodded and rose, pulled on clothes, and paused at the door. "I'll meet you at the arch."

"I'm going alone," he said. "I don't know what kind of reaction I'll get."

"I'm going with you. He can tell you anything, any kind of excuse with a religious half-truth. You won't know. I will," she said, and he turned her words in his mind.

"Under the arch," he said, and she hurried from the room. He lay back and pulled sleep around himself, the tiredness in his back and shoulders making that an easy task.

The sun was bright when he woke, freshened up and dressed, and rode to the iron arch. Isabel arrived a few minutes later, managing somehow to look fresh as a new bow. She rode beside him in silence to the mission, and as they dismounted in the courtyard, Father Junípero appeared with his hood thrown back.

"Good morning." He smiled. "A surprise visit. I enjoy surprise visits."

"Maybe not this one," Fargo said. "Where can we talk?"

With a lift of one eyebrow, Father Junípero led them into the mission and a small, square room with no furnishings except for a small pew in one corner. He turned to Fargo, his long, lean face with an expression of calm curiosity that bordered benign amusement.

"Did some shoveling last night," Fargo began. "Up on the hill." The calm curiosity gave way to surprise. "Father Antonio and two of the brothers," Fargo said calmly.

"Are you saying what I think you are?" Father Junípero said, incredulousness in his voice.

136

"I am," Fargo said.

"You went to the cemetery? You dug up graves?" the priest asked, shock replacing incredulousness in his voice.

"Bull's-eye," Fargo said.

The priest stared at him openmouthed. "You violated the sanctity of the grave? My God, my God. That's desecration," he said. "Why, my dear man? Why? What could make you do such a terrible thing?"

"Terrible curiosity," Fargo said. "And you know what I found? They hadn't died of food poisoning. Or maybe you knew that already."

Father Junípero met Fargo's hard-eyed gaze as the shock stayed in his face. He made no reply for a long moment and then drew a deep breath and let the sigh slowly spill from his lips. "Yes, I knew that," he said. "You found they died of gunshot wounds. Technically, at least."

"What's that supposed to mean?" Fargo growled.

"I had them shot," Father Junípero said, and Fargo felt his own brows lift at the unexpected admission. "It was against everything the Church stands for, a sin of the worst kind, but I did it. If you could have seen their agony, their suffering, and heard their screams of pain. Mushroom poisoning is apparently a horrible death. I obeyed their pleas. I knew the sin of it. I knew all that I was violating. But I told myself it was a higher mercy to do it."

Isabel's voice cut in. "Keeping guns at a mission is not proper," she said. "How did you come to have a gun?"

"I didn't. I hired a man, paid him out of our modest funds. He earned his pay and left at once," Father Junípero explained. "I have confessed my act in my prayers every day. I ask for absolution for my grievous sins. I am a man cast down upon himself. I must pray for forgiveness all my life, and I will never know, until that final time, whether it has been given me. This is my burden to carry for the rest of my days," he said, and blessed himself.

Fargo shot a glance at Isabel and she returned a half-shrug of uncertainty and a frown of confusion.

Father Junípero's voice broke into the silent exchange. "Now you know everything. You are the only two living souls beside myself who know. Not even the brothers know. Everyone was wrapped for burial when they arrived. I can only pray for your forgiveness, too," he said, and lowered his head.

Fargo swore under his breath as the man's answers swirled through his head, and another glance at Isabel gave him no help. He needed time to sort out what he'd been told and his own churning thoughts. "That's a hell of a goddamn story, I'll say that," he bit out, and Father Junípero looked up at him.

"I suppose blasphemy is of little consequence after desecration," the *padre* said reproachfully.

"You're right there," Fargo said. "I'll be in touch." He turned and strode from the room, with Isabel on his heels.

"Bless you both," Father Junípero called after them, and Fargo swore inwardly as he climbed onto the pinto and rode from the mission at a fast canter. Isabel caught up with him as he was halfway down the hillside and he slowed the horse to stare at her.

"You wanted to come along. You wanted to make sure he didn't give me some phony excuse. What the hell do you think now?" he threw at her angrily.

"I don't know. He didn't make any mistakes from a religious standpoint," she said. "It's a perfectly believable story, especially the way he tells it."

"Yes, full of guilt and contrition." Fargo frowned.

"That's certainly understandable. He violated all

the chief tenets of his faith and his vows. I'd expect he'd be full of guilt and contrition," Isabel said.

Fargo pulled to a halt at a small shaded circle of blue spruce and slid to the ground, his lips a thin line, his thoughts racing, and he felt Isabel come to stand beside him. "You saying you believed him," he tossed at her.

"I'm saying I can't find any reason not to, in what he said," she answered.

"That's the same as saying you believe him."

"Not quite but almost."

Fargo stared into space as thoughts continued to swirl through his head. Isabel waited silently beside him. Suddenly he turned, his jaw tight. "No," he snapped out, and drew a surprised glance from her. "It's too damn believable, everything in place, even the guilt and contrition. So was his story about finding everyone dead or nearly dead from mushroom poisoning. Every story he tells is believable, no loose ends anywhere. The ones who died can't talk, and now he says the others arrived too late to know about his mercy killings. It's all too damn neat."

"Truth is often neat," Isabel said.

"It's often sloppy, too."

"Do you think he's a priest gone mad, a lunatic in Franciscan robes?"

"Maybe and maybe not. What about all the errors and omissions you caught in his Mass? And Brother Rolando was killed on his way there," Fargo reminded her. "He was expected and he never reached the mission."

"What are you getting at?"

"I've been saying that gang of killers had a front man, someone the ranchers knew and trusted, the way Hod and Dora trusted their visitor. Maybe I was wrong about it being one of the ranch managers. A friar would be someone everyone would trust and welcome," he said, and Isabel stared at him, her black eyes wide.

"Father Junípero is not a priest gone mad? The friars are the bandits?" she breathed.

"I don't know, but the more I go over everything, the more it looks that way, even to those damn horses they keep for sale. Maybe not for sale. Maybe for hard mountain riding. I remember when I stopped by the day after the attack on the cross, the horses had all been brushed down. 'A healthy horse is a happy horse,' the good father said," Fargo recalled with a bitter grunt. "I'm going to find out once and for all."

"How?" she asked as he climbed onto the Ovaro.

"Have a real look inside that mission," he said.

"How are we going to do that?" she asked as she rode along.

"*We* aren't going to do that," he told her. "Magdalena's going to get me inside."

"You can't cut me out now. That's not fair."

"Fair's got nothing to do with it. You don't know your way into the mission any more than I do, but Magdalena used to play inside all the tunnels as a child while Pedro helped build the place. She's the only one who can get me in."

"What makes you think she'll do this any more than she'd help you dig up graves?" Isabel tossed back.

"This is different."

"Suspecting the brothers of being thieves and killers will be the same thing to her. It's not a thought she could handle."

"I won't say that. I won't put it that way. I'll give it a different face. I'll convince her," he said.

Isabel tossed him a narrow-eyed glance and said nothing more till he halted under the iron arch at the ranch. "When are you going to do this convincing?" she asked.

"Tonight."

"Make sure you use only words."

"You misjudge me," he protested.

"Hah," she snapped as she rode on.

He'd do whatever he had to do to enlist Magdalena's aid. Isabel knew that, too, damn her gorgeous hide. He turned the pinto around and set off back into the hills.

# 8

Fargo stayed high on the hill, hidden in a thicket of gambel oak, until the day neared an end. He had watched the mission below, waited and wondered, and had seen no unusual activity of any kind. The brown-robed figures crossed and recrossed the courtyard in pairs or in long rows. Sometimes they carried small sacks of flour into the building, sometimes they tended a small vegetable garden in one corner of the grounds. If Father Junípero had been unnerved by what had happened during the morning, there were no outward signs of it. If the friars were not what they seemed to be, there was no outward sign of that either.

But then, cleverness and caution had been a hallmark of the bandits, he reminded himself as he turned the Ovaro down the hill and rode into the gathering darkness. The night was full when he arrived at Magdalena's. He had taken the time to sleep some and to compose his approach to Magdalena.

She opened the door when she heard him arrive and was clinging to him almost at once. "It is late. I was about to go to bed," she said. "Now you can go with me."

"That's not why I've come, Magdalena," he said. "I need your help."

"My help?"

"I've got to get inside the mission, down into the cellars," he said, and saw the instant dismay come into her face.

"You want to do something bad again?" she said. "I will not help you desecrate."

"No, no, nothing bad. I have learned things that make me think that the friars may be in danger."

Magdalena's eyes widened. "In danger?" she echoed.

"I think the *bandidos* have found a way into the mission, and the friars do not know this," he said, choosing words carefully. He saw concern replace dismay in her face. "That's why I have to get inside. I have to see things for myself. But I don't want to alarm the friars or let the *bandidos* know. They may be watching the mission. You said you know all the tunnels inside the mission. You played in them as a little girl when Pedro was helping build them."

"Yes, I do."

"Then get me inside."

"When?"

"Tonight. Time is important."

"All right. Just let me put on a sweater," she said, and he nodded and felt miserably traitorous. She got the mare from the shed and rode beside him as he stayed in the heavy spruce cover until they drew opposite the mission. He swung to the ground and watched her peer at the silent, dark outline of the buildings.

"We go on foot from here," he said.

She nodded and they began to move toward the end of the rear wall of the courtyard. He held her back before she moved into the open land between the trees, his eyes searching the darkness until he was satisfied that no brown-robed figures roamed the night. He took his hand from her arm and she hurried to the far corner of the rear wall, knelt to the ground, and began to push against a stone. He knelt beside her, added his strength, and the stone moved. He pushed harder and the stone moved again, inward, finally sliding back far enough for a figure to crawl through.

"It has not been moved for many years," Magdalena whispered as she followed him into a dank, narrow passageway, too low for him to stand up straight. "Follow it to the end," she said, and he moved forward in a half-crouch.

The passage came to an end at a tunnel, taller and wider, with earth walls. He straightened up. Torches set in wall holders burned at intervals down the tunnel, affording light to let him see the other tunnels that bisected the one they were in.

Magdalena pushed ahead of him and he followed her as she moved down the tunnel, turning into the second one that cut across, and hurried through it. "We are in the cellar now," she said. "There is a big storage room at the end of this tunnel."

He saw at least six more tunnels branch off from the one they followed, each illuminated with the flickering light of the wall torches.

"Why so many tunnels?"

"When the mission was first built, this was a wild land. The brothers wanted places to hide. Sometimes Indians attacked them. Sometimes just those who hated them," Magdalena said. "They also wanted the tunnels in place so they could build more rooms down here, a wine cellar, rooms to store grains. They were never built, though." She turned at another bisecting tunnel, and Fargo saw the wide space at the end of it and hurried forward. The tunnel emptied into a square, earthen walled room where shovels, hoes, rakes and wheelbarrows were piled in disarray. He felt the stab of disappointment and Magdalena's eyes on him.

"Is there another room down here?" he asked, and she nodded and hurried down the tunnel to the right. The passageway curved, straightened, and he found himself imagining that this was what the ancient monasteries of Europe must have been like, only with more elaborate catacombs in which to hide both the living and the dead.

The second wide room appeared at the end of the tunnel and he hurried into it with Magdalena, his eyes narrowing at the small mound in the center covered with canvas and burlap.

He strode to the covering, began to pull it away, and heard his soft cry of satisfaction as he took in the mound of gold, coins, silver, and atop it all, the sparkling precious gems from the great cross of Saint Mary's. He glanced at Magdalena as she stared frowning at the array of riches and lifted her eyes to his.

"I don't understand," she murmured. "This is all that has been stolen: money, gold, jewels. How have they hidden it here? I do not understand."

"You will now, my dear," a voice said, and Fargo spun, the Colt in his hand instantly. He saw Father Junípero step from one of the other tunnels, the hood of his brown robe thrown back. "Drop the gun or you're a dead man, Fargo," Father Junípero said.

Fargo heard the double click of two hammers being cocked. He lowered the Colt as he half-turned and saw the two brown-cloaked figures standing at the entrances to the two other tunnels. Both had six-guns leveled at him, and he cursed silently as he let the Colt slip from his fingers.

"Step back from it," Father Junípero said, and Fargo moved alongside Magdalena. "Keep him covered," the priest said as he undid the cincture of his robe and pulled the garment off to reveal Levi's, a shirt, and a holster underneath. The sandals were a jarring, mocking note. The man brought his gun up, to level it at him as the other two brown-robed figures shed their garments and only their sandals echoed what they had been but seconds before.

Fargo glanced at Magdalena and saw her mouth open, shock and horror in her face.

"Terrible, isn't it?" Father Junípero said. "Men of God turned killers and thieves. Shatters the soul, doesn't it?" He laughed, a high-pitched, cackling sound as Fargo saw his cynical words mirrored in Magdalena's horror-stricken eyes.

She stared at the three men and the brown robes that lay at their feet, and Fargo suddenly knew this was what Pedro had seen—the friars shedding their robes, their gun belts underneath, perhaps some of the stolen booty in their hands. It had been an enormity too shattering for Pedro to cope with, his trust, his faith, his beliefs, the core of his world smashed before his eyes. That's why he had fled in speechless shock, too overcome to give words to what he had seen.

And the very same shattering shock gripped Magdalena's face now, he saw. "*El diablo*," she gasped out. "*El diablo.*"

The one who'd called himself Father Junípero laughed again. "That's right, my dear. The devil. He called us, took us away from God. He won. He always wins," the man said.

Magdalena brought her hands to her mouth as if to stifle the cry of anguish inside her even as she continued to stare at the three figures in front of her.

"No," Fargo spit out. "It's not the devil's work. They're not men of God turned bad. They never were.

146

They're a bunch of stinking killers. That's all they are. That's all they ever were."

But Magdalena was beyond listening, wrapped in the trauma of her own shattered world. The scream burst from her as she whirled and raced into the tunnel. "Get her," the leader shouted, and the other two men raced after her. But the man's gun had lowered in the moment of distraction. Fargo dived, slammed into the man's knees as the shot went over his head. The figure went down with him, and he got his hand on the man's wrist. He had just started to twist when he glimpsed the half-dozen brown-robed figures materializing from one of the other tunnels. He tried to roll away, but a blow came down on his head and he saw flashing lights and felt himself sprawl on the ground. The flashing lights went away and there were hands pulling him to his feet, and the room and the flickering torchlight came into focus again. Three brown-robed figures held him as the other two that had chased Magdalena were dragging her back to the room.

They flung her on the ground as the one who'd called himself Father Junípero pushed to his feet with a glare at Fargo. "I'll get to you," he rasped, and turned to Magdalena. He offered a mock bow. "You should've listened to your friend here. Juan Escobar is the name, not that you're going to tell anybody." Magdalena stared at him, her eyes still filled with shock. "You see, we'd been looking for something different, something safe and full of opportunity, you might say. We watched these friars and saw how everybody liked them, trusted them, welcomed them. The rest just came to me, nice and simple. After I got rid of the real friars, the boys took their places. I found a book on conducting the Mass and reading Latin. That was the hardest damn part of it."

"I'll bet," Fargo grunted. "You should've worked harder at it. I wouldn't be here now if you had."

"Shut up," Escobar snarled, and returned his eyes to Magdalena. "We're going to send you to meet up with your Uncle Pedro," he told her. "But not until the good friars here enjoy you. They haven't been near a woman in a long time. Rules of the order, you know." His cackling laugh rose at his own little joke, and he stepped toward Magdalena. "Me, first." He smiled. "Seeing that I'm the priest here. Got to do things in accordance with proper Church etiquette." He laughed again and reached down, took hold of Magdalena's sweater, and pulled it over her head. Fargo saw his eyes widen in anticipation as they roamed over her deep breasts.

"Leave her alone, you lousy scum," Fargo said, and the man immediately turned to him, his face darkening.

"You looking to get yours first?" Escobar threatened.

"First, last, doesn't make much damn difference, does it?" Fargo returned.

"This way you can watch," Juan said, and laughed again.

"I'm not going to learn anything from a hairball like you," Fargo said as he tried to get the man to explode. He wanted to force a distraction, a moment when Magdalena could run again and perhaps make it this time. Escobar stepped toward him, his thin face growing dark and his lips twitching. But he held himself back.

"Later for you, mister," he said, and turned back to Magdalena. He reached down, started to yank her blouse open when the shot rang out, reverberating through the tunnels as though it were a cannon blast.

Fargo felt one of the brown-robed figures holding him release his grip, and the man pitched past him as blood spattered from a hole in his neck. The others

**148**

also let him go in an instinctive reaction as they dived to the floor. Another shot exploded, and Fargo saw Escobar roll behind the mound of coins and other booty. A third shot almost slammed into another of the brown-robed figures as the man half-ran, half-stumbled across the room.

Fargo spun, took two long strides, and tore the nearest wall torch from its cradle. He smashed it into the floor, where it went out in a shower of sparks to plunge half the room into dimness.

"This way," he yelled at Magdalena as he raced for the nearest tunnel, but she was already fleeing down one of the other tunnels. He scooped up the Colt where it lay and flung himself sideways as a shot from behind him missed his ear. He charged down the tunnel as the slender, willowy shape stepped from a niche in the wall, a rifle in her hands.

"What the hell are you doing here?" he flung at her as Isabel ran beside him.

"Saving your neck. Aren't you going to say thank you?"

"I'll tell you when we're out of here," he snapped as they reached the end of the tunnel and dashed down the one that opened on the right. Two brown-robed figures appeared at the end, and Fargo fired two shots and both men collapsed alongside each other. But two bullets had slammed into the wall near the Trailsman's head and he ducked and pulled Isabel down with him. He spun, saw three more robed figures charging down the tunnel after him, and he fired. One dropped with a groan while the other two dived away. "How'd you get here?" he asked as he ran again with Isabel.

"Followed you," she said. "I got lost in these damn tunnels. Didn't get straightened out till I heard the voices."

The tunnel ended and two more branched out, and as he peered down the one on his right, he saw the brown figures appear at the end. He yanked Isabel with him as he raced down the tunnel to his left.

"This place is a damn maze," she muttered.

"And I don't know where the hell we are," he growled, and his lips drew back in a grimace as he wondered about Magdalena. She knew her way through the labyrinth. She could avoid her pursuers, he hoped. The tunnel widened, opened onto the storage room with the shovels and hoes. "I think we're going in the right direction," he said as he started across the room. He'd reached the tunnel on the other side when Magdalena's scream echoed through the twisting passage. He came to a halt. "Damn," he swore. She had made a mistake, taken a wrong turn.

"Fargo," he heard Escobar call. "Come out or I blow her head off right now."

"Don't come," Magdalena shouted. "Run. Save yourself." Her words were cut off by the sharp sound of a slap. They were at the end of the tunnel to his left.

"Thirty seconds, Fargo," Juan called. "Bring the other bitch with you." No empty bluff, Fargo knew, and he met Isabel's eyes.

"Getting yourself killed, too, won't help her any," Isabel said.

"I can't leave her. Maybe they'll make a mistake. Maybe I'll get another chance," he said. "I can't just walk away."

"No, that wouldn't be you," Isabel said, bitter resignation in her voice.

"You run. Find your way out of here."

"I'll ride back and get help."

"That'll take too long. You don't come and they'll figure that's what you're doing. They'll clear out."

"Then I'm not walking away, either."

"Get outside, into the trees. Start shooting when they come out," he said. "Kind of a repeat performance, only better."

"What makes you think you'll be with them when they come out?" she asked.

"Until they make their getaway, we'll be worth more alive as hostages," he said. "Escobar is smart. He doesn't know what he might face outside. He'll want insurance. Now get out of here, dammit."

She turned, her lips tight, and he waited another few precious seconds as she hurried down the tunnel. "I'm coming," he called out, and started to slowly walk into the other tunnel.

"Hands in the air," Escobar shouted, and Fargo obeyed. When he reached the end of the tunnel, he saw the cluster of figures still in their brown robes, Juan and two others without their disguises. Magdalena looked at him, tears in her eyes, and he tossed her a grin.

"I always wondered what the old martyrs felt like," he said. "Decided to find out."

"Where's the other bitch?" Escobar barked.

"I don't know. She took off on her own when we split up. I'd guess she's outside by now," Fargo said.

Juan considered the answer. "Maybe," he grunted. "And maybe she's hiding down here someplace." He turned to the others. "We can't take the time to search the whole goddamn place for her. If she got out, she'll be hightailing it for help. Bag everything. We're getting out of here."

While two of the brown-robed figures held him and a third pressed a gun into Magdalena's side, the others shed their robes and began to throw all their loot in burlap sacks. It took them at least fifteen minutes to finish, and when they did, the last of them flung their robes off.

Escobar marched Fargo from the cellar, a gun pressed into his back, while another of the men dragged Magdalena along. They reached the chapel and hurried outside, where one of the men brought the line of horses and others carried saddles from inside the mission. "You didn't walk all the way here," Escobar said. "Where are your horses? We haven't time to pull you along."

Fargo nodded toward where he and Magdalena had left their mounts outside, and one of the men hurried out and returned with both horses moments later. Where the hell was Isabel? Fargo muttered to himself. He'd expected her to be shooting by now. One of the men half-lifted Magdalena onto her horse and motioned to Fargo to mount.

Fargo swung onto the Ovaro and saw at least three six-guns trained on him. Each of the men, including Escobar, carried a burlap sack tied onto his saddle horn, he noted.

"Let's go," Escobar rasped, and led the way out of the courtyard. Two of the others flanked Fargo and another rode behind Magdalena. The rest were bunched together.

Dammit, what happened to Isabel? Fargo swore in silent alarm, a sinking feeling gathering in the pit of his stomach.

Juan Escobar turned east along the one wall of the mission, and he had just cleared the corner when the rifle shots exploded. One of the two men flanking Fargo flew from his horse, and Fargo saw another two topple as the shots continued to resound.

He reached down to his calf and yanked the double-bladed, razor-sharp throwing knife from its calf holster as the others wheeled their horses in momentary confusion. He pulled the pinto against one of the other horses, saw the man turn and start to yank at his gun. It never cleared the holster as Fargo's arm lashed out with the speed of a rattler's strike, and the thin blade plunged into the base of his throat.

Isabel had stopped firing, probably to reload, but he heard the staccato bark of pistol fire and dived from the saddle as two shots came within a fraction of an inch from his head. He hit the ground as more shots rang out, and he felt his insides seem to tear apart as he heard Magdalena's gasped cry of pain. He looked up as she hit the ground, a round red stain instantly spreading across her blouse.

"Son of a bitch," Fargo rasped as he saw the man in the saddle beside Magdalena's mare, the six-gun still aimed at her. Fargo rose, charged forward even as he hurled the throwing knife with all his strength.

The man tried to bring his six-gun around, but the knife hurtled into his chest to the hilt. He trembled, stayed trembling in the saddle for a long moment, and then toppled to the ground.

Isabel had started firing again and Fargo saw two of the figures who tried to race away go down. He whirled to glimpse Escobar disappearing into the spruce. He flung a glance at Magdalena. She lay still on the ground, the red stain slowly spreading. Flinging curses into the wind, he pulled the Ovaro around and sent the horse racing after Escobar.

Fargo charged into the spruce and heard the man ahead of him racing headlong as he dodged trees in the moonlight that filtered through the spruce needles. The Ovaro closed ground, its surefooted power able to skirt the trees more closely, picking up precious seconds each time.

Escobar heard him coming and Fargo drew close enough to see the man look back, raise his gun, and fire a shot that was wild. Suddenly Escobar swerved to his left, straightened out, and Fargo followed to see him plunge into a dense thicket of hawthorn and mountain brush. He followed, heard Escobar's horse come to a stop, and he dived from the saddle as two shots slammed into the tree to his right.

The Trailsman crouched on one knee, straining his ears, and he picked up the careful sounds of Escobar as the man moved through the brush. He stayed in place, silent as a lynx lying in wait for its prey, letting his wild-creature hearing become his eyes.

Escobar moved closer, halted, listened, then moved on again. He was edging closer, cautious but confident.

Fargo remained motionless, hardly breathing. He'd have but one chance, he realized. He had to make it count. The brush rustled again, closer, to his right and he suddenly glimpsed the dark bulk of Escobar's figure.

He stayed on one knee, watched the man move closer, and caught the glint of a sliver of moonlight on a gun barrel. Juan halted, listened again, and Fargo knew the man cursed inwardly as he failed to hear his foe. Escobar moved forward, at an angle that came toward him, and Fargo continued to wait on one knee until Juan was hardly more than six feet from him. Fargo rose then, his body bent forward, fingertips touching the ground, as though he were a runner at the starting line. Juan took another step forward, directly in front of him now, and Fargo saw the man stop, slowly peer to his right and then his left. The man's instincts sensed danger close at hand, Fargo knew, and he waited another second, not daring to breathe, until Escobar turned his head away to peer into the brush on the other side of him.

Fargo sprang forward, using all the power in his leg muscles. The brush only rustled, but it seemed to crackle as though it were a roaring fire. Escobar spun, brought his gun up, but the figure barreled into him in a headlong tackle. Fargo felt the shot graze the top of his shoulder as Juan went down. He tried to bring his fist around in a downward blow as he landed half atop the man, but he saw the fake priest manage to bring the gun around. With a curse, Fargo flung himself sideways as the bullet ripped through his sleeve. He hit the brush and rolled as another shot slammed into the ground and he saw Escobar had regained his feet and charged forward, firing as he came. Two more shots plowed into the ground, one grazing Fargo's back, and then he heard the sound of a hammer hitting against an empty chamber.

He turned, sprang to his feet as Escobar charged and felt the barrel of the gun slam down on his skull. The world swam away for an instant, and he knew he pitched forward onto his hands and knees. He shook his head and the world swam back into focus but only in time for him to glimpse the kick that caught him in the chest. He went sprawling sideways as breath exploded from him; he landed on his back and saw Escobar come in with the gun upraised to slam it down on him again. There wasn't room enough for him to kick high, so Fargo shot his leg out in almost a straight line, his foot slamming hard into the man's knee. Escobar's leg buckled and the blow he brought down went sideways. Fargo rolled and managed to fling an arm out and smash it against the man's head. He spun and pushed to his feet to see Escobar trying to rise as his knee buckled again.

Fargo smashed a downward blow that caught the man across the bridge of his nose, and Escobar cursed in pain as he fell backward. "Goddamn, stinking bastard," Fargo shouted, Magdalena's red-stained form swimming into his mind. He sprang forward to smash another blow into the man's bleeding face when he caught the glint of the knifeblade. Twisting his body in midair, he avoided coming down atop Juan and the knife, hit the ground and spun, and pushed to his feet. Escobar was charging, the knife outstretched, his face running with the blood from his shattered brow bones.

Fargo ducked the onrushing figure, saw the knife pass his shoulder, and swung a roundhouse right from a half-crouch. The blow caught Escobar in the midsection and Fargo heard the man's breath rush from him as he doubled over. He came down on one knee, still trying to draw in breath, and Fargo's kick caught him flush in the ribs. Escobar went down sideways with a grunt of pain, managed to find his feet, the knife still clutched in his hand. But Fargo's blow slammed into his jaw as he straightened up, and he went flying backward to hit the ground. Fargo charged after the man, saw him try to roll away, and leaped into the air. He came down with both feet in the small of Juan's back and heard the man's strangled cry of pain.

Escobar shook as he lay facedown on the ground, and Fargo heard a rasping wheeze gurgle from the man's lips. He used his foot to push the man onto his side and saw the knifeblade embedded deep into his stomach. As Escobar gave a last twitch and lay still, Fargo drew in a deep breath. The victory was as bitter as it had been hard, and he made his way through the trees to where he had left the Ovaro. He pulled himself onto the saddle and realized he was bleeding from assorted cuts and scrapes.

As he rode back to the mission, the new day was sliding over the mountain peaks of the Sierras. When he reached the scene, nearly a dozen figures lay strewn across the ground. He saw Isabel sitting beside Magdalena's prone, still form.

He dismounted and Isabel's eyes lifted to his, wet

with tears. He reached down and pulled her to her feet. The sun began to spread across the ground, but even its gold warmth was unable to soften the stark horror of the scene.

"Three of them got away," she said.

"I got Escobar," he said, and walked to the Arabian with her.

"I'll send help."

"I'll wait here," he said as she climbed onto the horse.

She rode away and he lowered himself next to Magdalena. With his hand resting against her hair, he sat unmoving, wrapped in his own bitterness. But the knot of horsemen and the light utility wagon finally appeared, Isabel riding beside her father.

"We'll take care of everything, Fargo," Philip Rogers said. "The Jesuits have sent a replacement priest to Saint Mary, Father Dolan. We'll hold the services there."

"The mission was her church. Her friends, her people, they're all here," Fargo said.

Rogers thought for a moment. "You're right. I'll see that Father Dolan comes here for the service," he said, and Fargo walked to the Ovaro and climbed into the saddle. He rode slowly and found Isabel beside him.

"You'll stay for the service," she said, the remark delivered with gentle command and expectation.

"Yes."

"What, then?"

"I'll be moving on."

"I want to go into the Sierras, into the high mountains," she said. "I want to feel cleansed. I don't want to go alone."

"You won't," he said.

"It's over. We have to go on," she said.

"Three got away."

"It's over," she said. "The Franciscan provincialate will be notified. They'll send another staff of friars. The mission will go on serving the people."

They reached the ranch and she leaned over, brushed his cheek with her lips, and he rode on until he found a place under a cluster of alders. He lay down, slept, crawled into his bedroll when night came, and stayed in the hills until it was time to make his way down to the ranch.

The silent lines of villagers walked to the mission and the fancy carriages rolled slowly. The Jesuit priest kept the service simple, and Fargo stood alone at the back of the chapel, the thoughts that had throbbed for days inside him still there. Would it have ended differently had he handled it another way? Could he have done differently without tipping off the fake friars? Would there have been time? Or was it meant to end this way from the very first?

The questions would never be answered, he realized, and they would never go away. In time they would lose their searing edge. In time . . .

Isabel came to him outside after the service ended. "I'll get my things," she said.

"I'll wait for you just past the arch," he answered. He was in the saddle, the Ovaro grazing on a patch of grainfield weed when she arrived. He led the way through the low hills and reached the Sierra highland as night came.

Isabel shared his bedroll, and her hungry wanting made the world recede, the touch of her flesh cleaving onto his a strangely wild peace, a reaffirmation of the immutability of life. When Isabel's body quivered on his, her breasts pressed into his face and her screams echoing into the night, he felt the release of her own pain and he held her tight.

The night passed in satiated slumber and the new day brought warmth and the tentative renewal of happiness. They spent the days in lazy exploring through the ponderosa pine, swam in the cool high-mountain lakes, and let the pleasures of the senses take over the nights. It was a good time, a cleansing time, and they rode a good way westward until finally, on a starry night, her last gasp of ecstasy over, Isabel pulled herself to a sitting position.

"I'll have to start back, come morning," she said. "Great-aunt Margaret is due for a visit. She visits only once a year, mostly to see me. I have to be there. I'm still her favorite little niece."

"Who has grown up." He smiled.

"The best way."

"We'll ride out of the mountains here and go back along the low hills. It'll save a few days," he said.

"I'm sorry it has to end," she said sadly. "It's over now, finally."

"Three got away."

"It's over, Fargo. Every end can't always be tied. That's the way it is sometimes. It's still over," she said, brought herself down to him, and was asleep in minutes in the crook of his arm.

When morning came, he led the way down out of the Sierras, into the low hills, and turned east. They made good time, slept soundly, and were in the saddle with the early dawn. The terrain leveled off some, flattened roads through hills of low ridges. They had just topped a ridge dotted with hawthorn when he yanked the Ovaro to a halt and the frown pulled at his brow.

Isabel stopped, followed his gaze as he stared at the three brown-robed figures moving along the roadway below, their white cinctures swinging as they walked single-file, heads bowed under their hoods.

"Maybe it's not them," she murmured. "Maybe it's three real friars."

"It's them," Fargo muttered, and heard the grim excitement in his voice. "If they hid out for a few days and spent part of the others in their damn robes, this is just about where they'd be." His hand on the Colt at his side, he stared down at the three robed figures, when a carriage came over a rise, a middle-aged man and a woman in a dark-green cut-under buggy with elliptic springs.

He saw the three robed figures come to a halt as the carriage rolled to a stop, and the man, well-dressed, tipped his hat to the monks. "Stay here," Fargo said as he sent the pinto downhill. The three friars were talking to the couple, their backs to him, when he saw one reach under his robes and yank out a Remington-Beals five-shot single-action pocket revolver.

He also saw the expression of shock on the faces of the man and the woman as they stared at the three friars. The men had their attention on the couple and didn't hear him until he had almost reached them. One turned and Fargo saw his eyes widen under the hood just as the other two turned to see him.

The big Colt was in Fargo's hands and he fired, three shots delivered with such speed they almost sounded as one. The three robed figures seemed to do a strange rigadoon as each staggered one way, then the other, before collapsing almost on top of one another. The Remington lay still clutched in the one's hand, and Fargo saw the couple tear their shocked eyes from the robed figures to stare at him.

"The Lord works in strange ways," Skye Fargo said almost cheerfully. "Peace be with you."

He wheeled the pinto in a tight circle and cantered back to where Isabel waited. "*Now* it's over," he said.

She nodded as she followed him along the ridge. But one part of it would never be over for her, she knew. She'd never forget the big man with the lake-blue eyes they called the Trailsman.

## LOOKING FORWARD!

**The following is the opening
section from the next novel in the exciting
*Trailsman* series from Signet:**

## THE TRAILSMAN #107
## GUNSMOKE GULCH

*Summer, 1860, in Colorado high country,
where a treacherous woman and worse men
were brought together at the end of a rainbow
and sweet revenge came quick . . .*

The big man astride the powerful black-and-white
pinto dug a silver compact out of his pocket. He had
taken it from Marie Mercier's clothing. The Louisiana
whore's naked and dead body lay where it had fallen
in the Mexico desert far behind him, a victim of the
Sharps, but not by his hand. Flipping the compact's
lid open, he studied the length and shape of his mustache and beard in the tiny mirror. Skye Fargo
decided both were all right. He snapped the lid shut
and returned the compact to his pocket. The piece of
jewelry was destined to belong to Miss Candy, who
owned the saloon at Wagon Wheel Gap in Colorado.
Candace liked to receive gifts, especially jewelry.

Fargo was headed due north, riding under a warm
sun. He was about ten miles inside New Mexico Territory, on the rutted trail that passed Clearview Hill.
Atop the lonely hill one could see for miles. He

decided to go up it and look around, stretch the kinks out of his muscular body, and let the stallion graze.

He faced south, and the rise offered him a majestic panoramic view of a vast expanse of the raw and still-untamed New Mexico Territory. Although a sunny day, he saw storm clouds building in the west.

Skye Fargo would be gone before the storm struck. He would be on the trail followed by wagon trains heading north to Beaver Pond in Colorado Territory. He whistled for the Ovaro, which had gone down the rise to graze. The stallion came immediately, with his ears perked.

"Good boy," Fargo whispered, rubbing the pinto's face. "Time for us to be moving on."

He eased up into the saddle and put the pinto at a walk. He passed the time by counting how many wagons left the fresh ruts. He concluded that seven Conestogas had made them.

Soon the scenery changed, to Fargo's liking. A stream off to his left gurgled as it rushed south over a rocky bottom; a woodpecker drilled for a worm in a dead tree; six doe, followed by the buck, crossed the trail ahead. He was in the mountains, in a narrow valley; blue spruce were everywhere as far as the eye could see, interrupted by slashes of golden aspen, their leaves quaking in the gentle breeze. An unseen elk whistled.

Rounding a bend, Fargo's wild-creature hearing detected a new sound, one that didn't belong to nature. He nudged the Ovaro to a lope and went to investigate.

In a small meadow were seven Conestogas, all overturned, six still smoldering. Bodies littered the ground. All had arrows in them. Riding in, Fargo heard a pain-filled groan. He dismounted instantly and began a search.

Coming to the overturned Conestoga that had not been torched, he spotted an old man sitting on the ground, his back against the wagon's underside. Three arrows protruded out of the old-timer's chest. The man's eyes were closed, and he was mumbling incoherently between painracked groans.

Fargo squatted next to him. In a flick of his eye he noted the depth and placement of the arrows. Fargo knew the tough old man was close to taking his last breath.

When Fargo coughed, the man's eyelids fluttered partway open, and he said with much effort, "The savage bastards took my Annie."

Looking around at the bodies, Fargo nodded. The old man found the strength to grasp Fargo's shirt and pull him nearer, then he whispered, "Find her, mister . . . find her. I'll pay you to find my Annie."

Releasing the shirt, his hands moved slowly to his own shirt pocket. The old man fumbled a small leather bag out of it, saying, "Open it, and you will see."

Fargo released the drawstring and dumped four nice-sized gold nuggets into his palm. He fingered them, looked at the old man, and asked, "What's your name, old-timer? Where did you get the nuggets?"

He wanted to ask more, but the old man cut him off. "Name's Roscoe Hogg. I got them from our mine, Charlie's and my mine. Charlie, he's my brother. The savages killed him." Roscoe paused to cough. Fargo heard a death rattle. Roscoe went on, "Find Annie and take her to the mine. Annie will pay you ten times this amount. Promise me you will find her." He started coughing again.

Fargo had to wait for Roscoe's coughing seizure to pass, then said, "I'll do my best to find her, I promise I will."

The old man relaxed, closed his eyes, and died.

*Excerpt from GUNSMOKE GULCH*

Fargo looked at the arrows, which he recognized as being Apache. He thought it odd their being in Colorado Territory, especially this close to the little town of Beaver Pond. He broke off one of the fletches and put it in his shirt pocket. Rising, he looked at the bodies again, then stepped to each. He counted seven men and four youngsters—three boys and a small girl—and two older women. He thought that odd, too, and went back and looked at the men's faces. Most were young. He guessed about twenty-five or so, no more than thirty.

Only one survivor, he told himself. Why did they take her? He looked at the old man and wondered if Roscoe had been mistaken. As far as Fargo and Hogg knew, Annie's body was one of the older women's. Hogg hadn't mentioned her age, whether or not Annie was his wife.

Fargo decided a promise was a promise. He would look for Annie. He picked up where the Apaches had left the massacre site easy enough and whistled the Ovaro to him. While waiting for him, he counted many unshod hoofprints, among which were five shod. He squinted to inspect the five. He concluded their depth meant only one thing: double riders. They had taken five women.

Mounting up, he began tracking the savages. They had gone west, crossed the main trail, and then turned south at a gallop. He found where the unshod ponies and the shod parted. The unshod riders went due south, the shod southwest. All led to New Mexico Territory. Fargo chose to follow the shod. After riding a short distance he found a piece of yellow gingham snapped on a thicket. Now convinced that they had captured women, he quickened the pinto's pace.

The first few drops of rain were big and cold. They dimpled the dry soil, but not enough to stop him.

Shortly the squall line unleashed its full fury, heralded by stiff wind, lightning, and thunder. Fargo watched the shod tracks disappear as the earth turned to mud. Further tracking was impossible. He turned and headed back to the massacre site.

He rode out of the squall a short distance later and found the meadow as dry as before. He dismounted and located a pick and shovel in one of the wagons. In an hour he had dug a shallow, common grave to hold the bodies. After lowering them into the grave, he put the shovel to work and covered them up. Leaning on the shovel's handle, he removed his hat and muttered, "Rest in peace."

Grim-faced, Fargo put on his hat, then got in the saddle. Facing south, he saw that half the sky was solid black with roiling storm clouds. The sky above him was clear. A warm sun beamed down on the big man as he cut between two of the overturned wagons and headed for Beaver Pond.

Crossing the meadow, he saw shod hoofprints where none should have been. He followed them to a stand of aspens that formed the tree line on the northern perimeter of the meadow. Just inside the grove there was a knoll. On top of it he saw where the rider joined up with seven others, all riding shod horses. The seven came from the direction of Beaver Pond. He followed their tracks down the rise. At the bottom, on bare earth, he saw a horse had thrown its left rear shoe.

Fargo proceeded to track the seven all the way to Beaver Pond, where the print of the horse with the missing shoe vanished among the many other hoofprints and wagon ruts.

He halted and sat easy in the saddle while looking down the one street of Beaver Pond. The little town had grown since he'd last seen it. He saw big Angus McCord's Trading Post was still standing, its sod-and-timber roof and log sides still in the process of rotting. One end of the roof sagged dangerously low.

Angus was the original inhabitant. The crusty, outspoken mountain man had named the place after the abundance of beavers' ponds in the area. Then he promptly killed all the beavers for their pelts.

In time, Bo Weathers built a small saloon facing McCord's place, just so they would have a street. McCord made Bo take it down and move it back a ways, claiming all the noise bothered his "peace and tranquillity." Bo had no idea what tranquillity meant, but wasn't about to argue with the rough-cut mountain man. Bo moved the structure.

Fargo saw the saloon had been widened to twice its original size. In addition to front windows, it now had a high false front with the new owner's name painted on it in big white letters: SALOON AND GAMBLING HALL, JACK CASTLE, PROPRIETOR.

A small hotel named Beaver Pond Hotel had also been erected since Fargo was last here. A fifty-foot gap separated the hotel from McCord's Trading Post.

And there was a blacksmith's place, complete with a livery, next to the saloon. Fargo heard the smithy pounding on an anvil, shattering McCord's peace and tranquillity.

Next to the livery stood a feed store, with several Studebaker farm wagons parked in front. Adjacent to the feed store was a small general store, and next to it a new sheriff's office and jail. They have need of a jail? Fargo thought.

He checked inside McCord's Trading Post and found it deserted. A few items hung on the walls, and the tables were filled with hides. Evidence that Angus was nearby. He looked at the horses hitched to rails in front of the saloon and walked the pinto over to them. He loose-reined the stallion to the rail, then began lifting the horses' left hind hooves. After finding all of them shod, he stepped to the swinging doors and paused to look inside.

Five men were seated around a table in the back corner, talking in low tones while sharing two bottles of whiskey from which they swigged often.

Six men stood at the bar, which ran the length of the saloon, each resting a boot on the wooden rail. A weasel-faced bartender stood behind the bar, wiping glasses.

Two other men occupied a table next to a window.

Nobody was gambling.

Fargo pushed through the double doors and moved to the end of the bar, where it turned and blocked access to the liquor. From there he could see everybody in the room. "Bartender, send down a bottle of bourbon," Fargo told him.

Instead, the man brought the bottle. Setting it in front of Fargo, he said, "That'll be two dollars." He held out one hand for the money, kept a grip on the bottle with the other.

Fargo asked, "Two dollars? What's in it? Gold dust?"

Weasel Face looked at him impatiently and replied. "Two bucks, stranger. Take it or leave it."

Fargo's right hand shot to the man's shirt. Pulling him nose-to-nose, Fargo slapped two silver dollars on top of the counter and growled, "I'm paying, but I don't like your attitude. Give me another of your snotty looks or tell me to take it or leave it, and I'll drag you over this counter and beat the shit out of you. Got that?"

Weasel Face gulped and nodded.

Fargo let go of the shirt and swilled from the bottle. The men at the bar ceased conversing and looked at Fargo. During the silence the Trailsman moved to stand at the far end of the bar. Looking at their reflections in the mirror, he studied the men at the table in the back corner. Four wore ripped and torn dusters, and they had unkempt hair and hands, wild looks in their eyes. Drifters, he decided, the very kind who would kill their mothers for a nickel. The fifth man, shorter than the others, and older, was bald and clean-shaven. He wore Levi's and a checked shirt that appeared clean. A Joslyn Army revolver rode low in the holster tied to his left thigh.

Fargo's wild-creature hearing eavesdropped their conversation. Baldy was saying, "You Barrow brothers did a fine job. Perfect, in fact. And I won't forget it."

Fargo watched them rise, shake hands, and heard the older Barrow say, "Money talks. We'll be there to help. Won't we, John?" He cut his eyes to John.

John answered, smiling, "You said it, Neal. What our big brother says goes for all of us. Right, Ray?" John glanced at the youngest man. "Right, Frank?" He poked the other man's arm.

"Fine," Baldy said. "Then let's head northwest."

As they were leaving, Fargo turned and rested his back up against the edge of the bar. In a loud voice, he said, "You men wait up."

They stopped in midstrides. Neal Barrow turned to face Fargo and motioned his brothers to spread out. Pulling his duster open, Neal's right hand settled in position to draw the Navy Colt from its holster.

Fargo's elbows were on the bartop, the bottle in his gun hand. Grinning, he raised both hands and said, "I'm not looking for trouble. I'm looking for help."

As he spoke, a man entered through the back door and stepped to the bar. He was followed closely by a skinny, stringy-haired brunette with sad-looking eyes. She wore a much-used and -abused, tight-fitting dress.

She glanced at Fargo and shot him a halfhearted smile, then proceeded to go behind the bar.

Fargo continued, "What I was about to say was, I came across a wagon train about five miles from here. Apaches massacred most of the people." He pulled the fletched part of the arrow from his shirt and laid it on the bar to show evidence. During his brief pause, in his peripheral vision he saw the bartender hurry out the back door. "Young children and older women were also killed. But I know the Apaches took at least five females with them when they headed south to New Mexico Territory."

"How do you know that?" Baldy asked.

"Because I tracked five sets of shod hoofprints. All five horses were carrying extra weight."

Neal Barrow chuckled. "That don't mean nothing. Ever hear of fat Apaches?" Neal's hand released the edge of his duster.

"Only thing is," Fargo began, "there was a survivor, an old coot—"

"His name?" Baldy interrupted.

"Roscoe Hogg," Fargo answered. "I found him dying. The tough old buzzard had three arrows in his chest, any one of which should have killed him instantly. Just before he died, he told me his name and that the Apaches had taken his Annie. So I know they took her, and probably other females."

"What prevented you from tracking them into New Mexico Territory?" the barrel-chested man at the table next to the window asked. "By the way, my name's Jack Castle. I own the saloon."

Fargo nodded, then said, "Look outside and you'll see what stopped me. Rain washed away all signs of their tracks. I'm going back to search for the woman. I'm asking for help. If we spread out where the rain halted me, the hunt for them will go much faster. Can I count all of you in on this?"

"Er, what else did the old man say before he died?" Baldy asked.

Fargo had a funny feeling about Baldy, spawned when he preceded the question with the "er." It was time for Fargo to hold back information. He said, "Not much. Like I said, I got to him as he was taking his dying breaths. He did mention that the savages killed his brother, Charlie, too. Other than that, he was concerned about Annie."

Baldy visibly relaxed.

Fargo was about to mention the other survivor who met seven riders on the knoll. Before he could say anything two powerfully built men came through the double doors followed by Weasel Face, who pointed a wavering finger at Fargo and said, "That's him, Sheriff. He's the one causing trouble."

Both the sheriff and his deputy drew their revolvers and aimed them at Fargo's chest. The sheriff snarled, "You're under arrest. Disturbing the peace in this town is a hanging offense."